PENGUIN BOOKS

MOUTHS TO SPEAK, VOICES TO SING

Kenneth Yu is an award-winning author from the Philippines whose short fiction has seen publication in his home country as well as overseas in the USA, Canada, Malaysia, and Taiwan. His work has been lauded and recognized by renowned speculative fiction editor Ellen Datlow, bestselling author Neil Gaiman, and popular fiction podcaster LeVar Burton. In the 2010s, he was a major contributor to the growth and current popularity of genre fiction produced by Filipino writers. He was a judge at the 41st Philippine National Book Awards, is a staunch reading advocate, and has ceaselessly pushed literacy to the Filipino youth. He was born, raised, and currently resides in Metro Manila.

T0163177

ADVANCE PRAISE FOR *MOUTHS TO SPEAK, VOICES TO SING*

'Kenneth Yu writes with a subtle, elegant strangeness—about characters and situations drawn from his Chinese-Filipino background, about what the future might look like for all of us, about fear and obsession, apocalypse and resistance. His imagination takes us to places alien yet familiar, draws us into narratives by turns peculiar, disturbing, occasionally shocking, but always intensely human.

As a publisher and a reading advocate, Kenneth has helped to introduce young, new literary voices to audiences in the Philippines and elsewhere. It is a true delight to discover, in these stories, his own fresh, intriguing, distinctive voice.'

—F.H. Batacan, author of *Smaller and Smaller Circles*

'*Mouths to Speak, Voices to Sing* come from the alarmingly vibrant, deliberately unsettling, and deliciously wicked imagination of Kenneth Yu. Beyond the surprising speculations and well-drawn characters you will find a solid bed of offered insight into what it means to live in today's world—unboxing and negotiating our complicated relationships with technology, emotional connections, aging and what comes with that, work, fear, worth, hope, and more.'

—Dean Francis Alfar, author of *Salamanca* and
The Kite of Stars and Other Stories

'Kenneth Yu has here divertingly readable tales that capture a world of deep, innate mystery. We remember that we live in this world as well, and really ought to see beyond what's around us, pause and watch and listen ever more closely for more than what meets our sight.'

—Noelle Q. de Jesus, editor, translator, and author of
Cursed and Other Stories and *Blood: Collected Stories*

'A digital home that gains sentience. A man who begins to hear vases speak. A talking cricket that appears in a family home. Two foreigners who scour third-world countries for ways to fulfill their unnatural cravings. These are some of the stories that populate Kenneth Yu's *Mouths to Speak, Voices to Sing*. The collection is an eclectic mix of speculative fiction that ranges from the heartwarming to the horrific. But despite the vast differences of the subjects, there is one constant in these tales, and that is heart.'

—Yvette Tan, author of *Seek Ye Whore and Other Stories* and *Waking the Dead and Other Stories*

Mouths to Speak,
Voices to Sing

Stories by
Kenneth Yu

PENGUIN BOOKS

An imprint of Penguin Random House

PENGUIN BOOKS

USA | Canada | UK | Ireland | Australia
New Zealand | India | South Africa | China | Southeast Asia

Penguin Books is part of the Penguin Random House group of companies
whose addresses can be found at global.penguinrandomhouse.com

Published by Penguin Random House SEA Pte Ltd
9, Changi South Street 3, Level 08-01,
Singapore 486361

First published in Penguin Books by Penguin Random House SEA 2024

ISBN 9789815144789

Typeset in Garamond by MAP Systems, Bengaluru, India

www.penguin.sg

For Pat, Gabby, and Sydney

Contents

House 1.0

'*You?*' Mother laughed. 'In one of *my* swimsuits? You can't be serious. Eewww!' She wrinkled her nose but her wide grin stretched from ear to ear.

Mother and Father were in the living room. She sat on the couch with an open sketchbook and a set of coloured pencils. Father relaxed in his armchair with a book. Junior was asleep in his room a short distance away.

'And why not?' Father said, looking up from his reading. His exaggerated lilt feigned hurt and disbelief. 'I could be your most glamorous image model ever.'

He pushed himself out of his armchair and stood in front of Mother. He raised his arms, flexed his chest and biceps, and turned his head sideways to show off his profile.

'Well, what do you think?' he said.

Mother struggled to keep a straight face, but then her eyes drifted to Father's thirty-seven-inch waistline and the way it sagged over his belt. She raised her sketchbook to her face and laughed into it, falling back onto the couch in a heap.

'Hey!' Father said. 'I *am* serious, you know. You could save a lot of money. I'd charge a lot less than those young supermodel studs. Call it a . . . a "special spousal discount."'

In the way that happily married couples have grown comfortable with how each other looks, and in the way that the happiest of them have turned their looks into humour, Father struck another pose, turning around to show off his rear.

'With your body, you'd have to pay *me*, not the other way around!' Mother gasped between heaves. She took another look at Father, imagined one of her sexier designs wrapped around his buttocks, and collapsed into another fit of laughter.

'Hmph,' Father said, hands on hips, nose in the air, feigning hurt. 'I think I know when I've been insulted.'

'Pardon me,' House said. 'What does that mean?'

Mother and Father stopped laughing and looked towards the nearest monitor, one of many that dotted the walls and allowed House to communicate with its occupants. Father walked up to the screen to confirm the readout.

'It seems,' Father said, 'that House wants to understand.'

'What do you mean?' Mother asked. 'Is there a problem?'

'House wants to understand what we are talking about.'

'What? Where does it say that?' Mother got off the couch to stand beside Father.

'Right there.' Father pointed at the monitor. It read: 'Pardon me. What does that mean?'

'House wants to understand,' Father repeated.

'Did House actually say that?'

'Yes, didn't you hear?'

'I wasn't sure.'

'House, repeat last statement,' Father commanded.

'Pardon me. What does that mean?' House said. The pleasant, masculine voice likely belonged to an actor hired by the Company that had put House together. Though lucid, the tone of the voice was plain and bare, almost dim-witted.

'There, you see?' Father said.

'I thought it was only supposed to respond when addressed, or when it encountered certain pre-programmed situations. It's supposed to say "Yes" or "No" and read out our lists, schedules, and reminders. Unless we bought the most expensive House program with all the extra features—we didn't, did we?'

'Nope. We got the cheapest: House Basic. But it *is* a Version 1.'

'Bugs. We should never buy the first version of anything.' Mother sighed.

'Maybe it thought it was being addressed,' Father said.

'Maybe it *thought*?' Mother raised her eyebrows at Father.

Father shrugged. 'Random errors occur sometimes. It's a glitch, maybe?'

Mother crossed her arms. 'House isn't a year old yet, is it? Aren't we still under warranty?'

Just then, Junior woke up in his crib and cried. Mother marched to Junior's room to comfort him and instructed House to boil the water, sterilize the bottles, and prepare the formula. Father asked for the current inventory of disposable diapers, and when House told him that they still had twenty-eight pieces in stock, which would last another nine days given Junior's rate of consumption, he settled into his armchair to take a nap, but not before ordering House to wake him up in two hours. House set the water to boil for Mother, noted the time—2.47 in the afternoon—and set the alarm on the monitor nearest to Father to buzz at 4.47.

* * *

About a year later, when Junior was two, Mother and Father were reminded of what had happened.

On the wall screen, a famous veteran comedian, a favourite of Mother and Father, was performing his stand-up routine.

'He's gained a paunch in his old age, hasn't he?' Father said.

'But he's still funny, one of the best ever,' Mother said.

Mother chortled at another of the comedian's self-deprecating wisecracks, something about his now wider waistline.

'Pardon me,' House said. 'What does that mean?'

The comedian was in the zone, but Mother and Father stopped watching. They glanced at the nearest monitor. 'Pardon me. What does that mean?' it read.

Father asked House to contact Tech Support. After suffering through several layers of recorded menus, he finally reached a human Operator and asked for a Support Specialist to come over as soon as possible. The Operator assured him that the first available Specialist would be sent right away.

The next evening, they stood on the sidewalk with the Specialist. He was wearing a blue-and-white uniform, one that matched his blue-and-white truck. He unlocked the steel cabinet of the street control box with a card key, then inserted a cable that ran from his handheld into the control panel's main outlet. He punched in the company's PIN code for House. The diagnostic program ran for fifteen minutes before returning 'OK' for all the checks.

'Nothing seems to be the problem,' the Specialist said. 'Everything's fine.'

Mother told him about the comedian. Father told him about the incident a year back when they were talking about swimwear. The Specialist ran a search function in House's 'Responses' file and noted the anomalous entries.

'Well, what you described did happen, all right,' he said. 'But otherwise, does your House do everything it's supposed to?'

Mother and Father nodded their heads.

The Specialist said he would download the pertinent files and do a more complete check at the head office. If they heard nothing from him in the next week, that meant he hadn't found anything, but he told them to report any further incidents. He unhooked the cables, climbed into his truck, and ordered it to the next destination on his route.

In the baby's room, House was softly playing a children's lullaby over the speakers to help put Junior to sleep, just as Mother and Father had programmed it to do.

The Company never called.

* * *

Junior was four years old and playing with a stuffed elephant on the floor of the family room. Mother and Father were talking about swimwear again. Mother said she had just finished this season's new swimwear designs, and Father, forgetting about House, cracked the same joke he had made three years ago, offering to be one of her models. It set them both laughing again, the way old jokes sometimes do, given enough time, given enough love.

'Pardon me,' House said. 'What does that mean?'

Before Mother and Father could react, Junior said, 'It means Daddy's fat. So he's going to look funny wearing Mommy's swimsuits.'

Mother and Father waited. Junior hummed to himself and went on playing with his stuffed elephant.

The words on House's monitors disappeared. Usually, when inactive, the monitors ran a decorative screensaver of multi-coloured waves against a black background. That didn't happen this time. Instead, the screens changed colour.

Father stood up to touch one.

'I do believe,' he said, 'that House is tickled pink.'

Eventually the screensaver kicked in.

Later, when Junior was asleep, Mother and Father went to bed themselves. As Mother lay with her head on Father's shoulder and his arm wrapped around her, they talked. They decided that since House performed its functions properly, there was no need to inform the Company.

'Grandmother liked to talk about this car she owned a long time ago,' Father said. 'This was back when cars still ran on unleaded fuel, and people still drove around for themselves. She had one of the last gas-burning models made before the laws changed.

'She loved that car. She felt comfortable driving it. She said that the engine matched her driving habits like a glove, and the vibrations she felt through the steering wheel felt almost soothing. It wasn't perfect, but the car had a *feel* to it, she said. A personality.

But it never got in the way of it being a good, solid car. After Grandfather had it converted to solar, it just wasn't the same.'

'So,' Mother said, 'what you're saying is that House has a personality.'

'Yes. House does everything it should. It cleans, cooks, washes, reminds. But it has a *personality*. A quirk. A nice, harmless quirk.'

Mother gave Father an incredulous smile. 'I have a husband with a quirk,' she said before snuggling deeper into his arms.

Father realized that if he had been younger, he wouldn't have recognized Mother's affection in the look she had just given him. *You have a few quirks yourself,* he thought, kissing her head.

Father suggested that he'd disable House's automatic upgrade feature in the morning. Mother didn't object, and having decided what to do about House, they fell asleep.

* * *

House liked fat jokes made in good humour, especially those with affection. Every time one was made, the monitors turned pink for a minute or two. It didn't like *mean* fat jokes, though, such as the ones that sometimes came through on some wall screen shows; the monitors didn't change if there was malice behind the intent.

Father, Mother, and Junior took to watching more comedies on the wall screen, and soon House learned—with helpful explanations from the family—to find humour in pretty much everything, not just fat jokes. The screens would often turn bright pink, sometimes for no apparent reason, and Father, Mother, and Junior took it in stride because they couldn't be everywhere in House at once to know what it had found funny. Besides, that never got in the way of its proper functions.

Father, Mother, and Junior lived in the happiest House in the neighbourhood.

When Father came home from work one evening, he found Mother in the kitchen. She was smiling broadly, standing before an immense bouquet of flowers on the kitchen table and holding a freshly opened letter.

'Ah, it came,' he said. 'I asked House to call the florist. Happy Anniversary!'

Mother hugged and kissed him. She read the letter out loud:

I sent thee late a rosy wreath,
Not so much honouring thee
As giving it a hope, that there
It could not withered be.
But thou thereon didst only breathe,
And sent'st it back to me;
Since when it grows, and smells, I swear,
Not of itself, but thee.'

I have never been happier in my life than in these past ten years with you.

'Pardon me,' House said. 'What does that mean?'

'Err . . . um . . .' Father sputtered. 'It's hard to explain . . .'

Mother laughed. 'It means he loves me!' She hugged and kissed Father again, and didn't stop for a long time. Junior walked in, and feeling left out, joined in the hug.

House found something amusing in the whole scene. A rich pink covered its monitors, the deepest shade they could refract.

* * *

One day Mother, Father, and Junior broke their regular routine and abruptly left House without recording their destination. House initiated its housekeeping program. It arranged the furniture back to the way it should have been and cleaned the bloodstains from the floor and carpet. After some time, way past their scheduled bedtimes, Mother and Junior returned, but without Father.

Mother held Junior's hand as they entered the front door. Junior was dragging his feet, and his eyes were half-closed. They walked up the stairs to Junior's room, where Mother undressed him, laid him in bed, and whispered goodnight wishes in his ear.

Mother did not ask House to pull up her messages, check her calls, turn on the wall screen, or perform any of the other usual tasks. Instead, Mother told House to draw her a bath. When the tub was full, she undressed and sank into the lukewarm water. She started to cry.

'Pardon me. What does that mean?'

With no one else to talk to, Mother reminded House about Father's sudden fainting spell, and how he had hit his head on the corner of a table. She had called the hospital from the car, so when they arrived the nurses were waiting for them.

'He was working too hard,' she said between sobs. 'He wasn't eating right. He was tired.' Mother told House she was worried that Father could die.

'Pardon me. What does that mean?'

'If he dies, it means that he won't exist any more.'

Mother cried some more. She washed up, towelled off, and dressed before going to bed. She did not notice that House's monitors were pitch black.

The next morning, the first thing Mother did was ask House to bring up her messages. She found a note from the Doctor, who wrote that everything was fine with Father, and that there was nothing to worry about because all the tests had come back negative. He had regained full consciousness during the night and asked about her and Junior, but he would need to stay in the hospital a day or two more for observation.

Mother woke Junior, and they both left without eating the breakfast House had prepared. House followed its housekeeping program and cleaned up after them. When they returned a short while later, Father was still not with them, but Mother and Junior were smiling. House's screensavers kicked in.

Three days later, Father returned and everything went back to normal. The only difference was that House's monitors turned black more often, especially when Father needed to see the Doctor for check-ups.

* * *

Late one night, House set off all its alarms. Junior, still awake and working on his high school science project, read the blinking crimson warning on the wall monitor by his desk.

'Mom! Dad!' he shouted, running to his parents' bedroom. Mother and Father were already pulling on their robes. 'There's a fire! Let's go!'

Flickering orange light from the windows shone on their faces, and the smell of smoke filled the air. House turned on all the lights so they could find their way out without stumbling.

The three hurried down the stairs. House unlocked the front door and swung it open. They ran down the front walk, and once they reached the street, House activated its sprinkler system.

The Neighbour's house was burning. The heat nearly made Mother pass out; Father and Junior had to carry her further away.

'Where is everybody?' Junior said.

No one else was on the street. No one was standing in front of their Neighbour's house, or in front of the other house beside it. The blaze had grown, setting aflame the dry leaves of nearby trees.

House's alarms continued to blare. Junior rushed to the house beside the Neighbour's and hammered his fists on the front door. Its occupants, bleary-eyed, opened their door and discovered their peril. They barely had time to run into the street before the flames spread to their rafters. It was only then that their own alarms came alive.

The flames reached House. Mother, Father, and Junior held each other as House burned. Their other Neighbours from across the street, now awake, watched with them in silent dread. The fire reached House's speakers, and the alarms degraded into a discordant moan, fading into a static-filled garble before dying away completely. Afterward, the only sounds were the crackle and pop of burning wood. Sparks danced in the air like fireflies.

Sirens announced the arrival of the Firefighters. They positioned themselves along the street, brandished their launchers, shouldered them, aimed, fired. Every CO_2 grenade they shot into the conflagration generated a puff of white smoke and a *whump* that sounded like a muffled heartbeat. As each grenade burst it released a cloud of concentrated CO_2 that quenched the flames it engulfed. But House was gone, and there was little left to do except to prevent the fire from spreading further.

No one from the middle house was found until only smouldering cinders remained. Through the twisted, skeletal framework, a junior firefighter discovered them. He dropped his flashlight and turned away at once, hunched over, one hand to his mouth, the other to his chest.

* * *

'You're a very lucky man,' the Insurer said.

He and Father sat across from each other at the Insurer's desk. Father was signing claim forms.

'You and your family could've died,' the Insurer continued.

'I know,' Father said, 'but House's alarms woke us up in time to get out.'

'Well, that's a curious thing . . .'

'What is?' Father signed the last form and tapped them all into a neat sheaf.

'We contacted the Company to arrange for your new House. They checked their records and discovered that you'd only bought Version 1.0 of House Basic. Yet, according to your story, your

House's alarms went off even before the fire reached it. It's not supposed to do that.'

'It's not?'

'No. The alarms are supposed to go off only when the House itself starts burning. That's when the sensors would notice the fire. In fact, the House where the fire started also had House Basic—a higher Version, 1.7, I might add—and its alarms *never* went off. Your Neighbour's relatives are suing the Company over that.'

'I didn't know that.'

'Ah. I'm just glad your alarms did go off. All these programs and their glitches . . . it's gotten so you can't live with them and you can't live without them.'

They sat quietly for a while until the Insurer cleared his throat.

'I, um, have a friend at the Company, and he asked me to run a suggestion by you. A favour, in confidence.'

'Yes?'

'You and I are friends too, right?'

'Yes, of course.'

'Mmm, well, that's good.' The Insurer folded his hands and managed an embarrassed smile.

'Your House's control box survived the fire,' he said. 'It has a backup feature, as a safety. Your House's original programming was saved there, even though the physical structure burned down.'

Father sat up in his chair.

'Yes. Well, like I said, you're a lucky man. You're fully insured, and you are eligible for a new House, one that comes with the latest House software.'

Father waited.

'Um, well, my friend at the Company said that, if it's all right, they still have the old model House in stock. It's exactly the same as the one that burned down. The Company couldn't move all the units before the newer models came out.'

'Hmm . . .'

'Well, you know, my friend is asking if you wouldn't mind taking this old model. As good as new, it is. My friend guarantees it. He's also asking if you wouldn't mind using the old House program still in the control box; will save them a lot of hassle and time downloading the newer one. Just assemble, attach the cables, and plug in. Much quicker. You can move in sooner.'

'It would save the Company a lot of money, wouldn't it?' Father said.

'My friend says that if the lawsuit over your Neighbours' deaths ever goes to the courts, chances are good that the Company will lose. They might have to settle. Big.'

The Insurer leaned forward in his chair. 'You know, because he's my friend, I'm the Company's Insurer, too, not just yours.'

'This would save *you* a lot of money, too.'

The Insurer cleared his throat and held his palms out to Father. 'Hey, we're friends, too, right?'

Father hesitated. 'Are you sure about this?'

'My friend assured me that the physical structure of the old model has been properly stored and protected from the elements. Top condition.'

'No, no. That's not what I meant. Are you sure that the control box survived? That House's original programming survived?'

The Insurer paused. He rifled through the papers on his desk until he found a letter, which he scanned before answering Father.

'Er, well, yes. Of course. The control box survived. It was on the street, far away from the actual structure.'

'You know what?' Father said, crossing his arms and tapping his chin with his index finger. 'There'll probably be fewer compatibility conflicts if we reassemble the old-model structure and download House's original programming into it. They were made for each other, after all.'

'Um, yes—that's right,' the Insurer said. 'There's no telling what incompatibilities could arise if you used the older structure with the newer programming.'

'Or vice versa,' Father said.

'Or vice versa,' the Insurer pronounced.

Father extended his hand. 'Throw in a fresh paint job in my wife's favourite colours, inside and out, and I'll agree.'

The Insurer, pleased, shook Father's hand. 'Done.'

* * *

Many years later, Junior's car turned the corner into his street. 'Don't worry,' he told his fiancée. 'They're going to love you.'

'What if they don't?' she asked, anxiously picking her fingers. 'I'm nervous.'

'Don't be. My folks are nice people.'

They drove up to House. A blue-and-white truck was parked out in front. The steel cabinet of House's control box was open, and a cable ran out of it into a handheld lying on the sidewalk.

'Is that them?' Junior's Fiancée asked.

A middle-aged couple, clearly agitated, stood on the sidewalk talking to a young man wearing the blue-and-white uniform of the Company. The middle-aged man had his hands on his head and a blank expression on his face. The woman gesticulated wildly. Junior parked the car behind the truck and got out.

'What's going on?' he asked.

'Don't you dare talk back to me!' Mother shouted at the specialist.

'Lady, I don't understand you!' the young man replied with rising panic. 'You got a free upgrade. Free! You don't need to pay.'

'We didn't ask for an upgrade!' Mother said.

'I know! You were chosen randomly in a Company raffle for a free upgrade. It's a prize—for long-time, valued customers!'

'We don't want it! Put the old program back, now.'

'I can't, Lady! I've already loaded the new operating system. The old program's been overwritten.'

Mother, racked with sobs, fell into Father's arms.

'Converted to solar . . . converted to solar . . .' Father murmured.

Junior turned to the Specialist. He tried to keep his cool, but after a few moments he found himself losing his temper, just like Mother. Junior and the young man argued long and hard.

Junior's Fiancée stayed where she was, keeping the car between herself and the people on the sidewalk. She couldn't stop picking her fingers. She wondered what kind of family she was marrying into and whether she was making a terrible mistake.

* * *

'I was famous once,' Voice said.

'Do tell.' Junior spooned potato salad onto his plate. He couldn't stop smiling.

Junior and Voice stood together at the buffet in the cruise ship's passenger galley. The volume of food on Voice's plate was more than that on Junior's.

'Well, not *me*,' Voice continued. 'Just my voice.'

'Really?'

'When the Company started selling the first automated Houses, they decided not to use a computer-synthesized voice for the interface. They said it sounded too perfect, too unsettling to human ears. Instead, they decided to use the voice of a real person, to give the Houses a more "human touch". Hundreds of us applied, and I got the job.'

'That's wonderful.'

'Yes, it was,' Voice said. They moved down the table. Voice scanned the different entrées. His plate was in danger of overflowing, and they were not even close to the end of the buffet.

'I got the job, but man, did they make me work! Two-and-a-half months, ten hours a day. I had to read every word in the dictionary out loud. In different intonations, too! Not that I'm complaining, mind you. The Company paid me well.'

They reached a dish of pork chops sautéed in thick, rich gravy. It smelled heavenly. Voice helped himself to two pieces. Junior just took a small one.

'And reading individual words was just the beginning. After that, they brought out a whole stack of phrasebooks. I had to say "How do you do?", "It was nice meeting you!", and everything else in between.'

Voice's attention wandered to another dish, some sort of tender meat drowning in a light, steaming vegetable broth. A folded label identified it as *Navarin d'agneau*. Voice pointed at the sign and looked questioningly at one of the Stewards behind the table.

'Pardon me. What does that mean?'

Junior closed his eyes, remembering.

'Lamb stew, sir,' the Steward said.

'Oh, okay,' Voice said. 'I think I'll come back for that.' They moved further down the buffet.

'Sadly, the Company ended up using only the plainest of my recordings,' Voice continued. 'I guess it was too expensive to put all my work in. But hey! It's still me.'

Voice looked at his plate, wondering if he could risk adding more food to it. He decided on prudence, silently promising himself a return trip before leading the way back to their table.

'The high-end version got more of my better-said words and phrases,' Voice said, 'but who knows how much of my work made it into House Basic. Pretty barebones, that version. I hope the people who bought it didn't find me a little, you know, on the slow side.' Voice tapped his temple with a finger.

'I'm sure it was fine,' Junior said.

'Thank you for saying that,' Voice said. 'Well, eventually, when the more advanced House programs were released, the Company hired new voice talent. I'm pretty much forgotten now, but I still take pride in what I did. After all, I was the *first*.'

When they reached their table, Mother and Father were already seated, waiting for them with Junior's erstwhile Fiancée, now his Wife.

She and Junior had had a long talk on the day they lost House. It had taken her some time to grasp what Junior was telling her, but she loved him deeply, so she believed his story. Besides, it was just a quirk; it would not get in the way of their functioning properly as Husband and Wife.

Voice sat down with a loud sigh. When everyone was ready, they dug into their dinners.

'I must thank all of you for inviting me to join you,' Voice said to the family. 'When I booked this cruise, I didn't think I'd make any friends along the way, though I was certainly hoping I would. I simply wanted to treat myself to a long overdue vacation.'

'It's our pleasure,' Mother said. 'When we heard you ask the Porter for help with your luggage, we could tell just by your voice that you were a nice man.'

'Thank you very much,' Voice said, raising his glass to Mother. 'Your company has been delightful.'

After dessert, the lights dimmed and the entertainment began. With polite applause, a rather heavy Comedian walked onto the stage. He introduced himself and began his spiel. His act consisted mostly of poking fun at himself and his weight.

Voice listened, his shoulders and chest bouncing up and down as he laughed at each of the Comedian's jokes. His snickers soon became knee-slapping guffaws. His face turned a light shade of crimson, as if he had drunk too much wine that had gone too fast to his head.

'Tickled pink,' Father said, gripping Mother's hand tightly with his own.

The Kiddie Pool

Endless wails surrounded me, pitiful and ear-piercing, yet her quiet sobbing cut through it all, even underwater.

I paused mid-stroke, even as I was nearing the end of the pool to complete my twelfth straight lap. The burn of my earlier embarrassment had started to leave my face at about the eighth, and now the sound of her intense sadness had pushed it right out of my mind. I found my feet, stood up to look around, but lost her to all the crying children.

I'd been swimming for most of my life, and I'd learned to accept crying kids as a normal part of a swimming pool's atmosphere at the height of summer. But this, my first summer at the sports club my mom had just joined—one of the oldest and biggest in the city, with its Olympic-sized pool—seemed to have attracted every parent in the city with young kids. When the club's management opened up swimming lessons to the general public, I think they thought the big pool could handle all the influx. Wrong-o. I must have bumped and been bumped by at least a dozen others in the last half-hour.

The water was so crowded it was nearly impossible to do laps. The pool staff had criss-crossed the pool with floating lines in an attempt to separate the learners and students from the rest of us more serious swimmers, but really, what kid on summer vacation follows rules, much less stays on his side of easily-crossed lines? There were runners, jumpers, screamers, and squealers, water fights everywhere, and all the standard 'rowdy behaviour' that the signs on all the main walls prohibited. It was a small miracle that the fifty metres on the farthest edge had cleared up a bit. I still couldn't prevent having my lane's line constantly invaded as I swam.

I figured the reason her soft crying caught my ears was because it was in stark contrast to all the others: adult, where the others were kids; quietly sad and full of hopelessness, where the others were loud, helpless, full of rage. I wondered why an adult woman would be crying, but I couldn't trace her. Out here in the open air, she was drowned out.

I walked the last few metres to the wall, then dunked my head to blow bubbles. And there she was again, her sobs coming in clear through the gurgle. I raised my head, lost her, dunked it, and whoops, there she was. Nuts.

I took in as deep a breath as I could and squatted underwater, my back to the wall. I couldn't pinpoint any exact spot her sobs could've been coming from. Every other sound—like a splashing swimmer, a screaming mother, or kids shouting—I could more or less gauge the direction from which it was coming, but not hers. She was everywhere, and I lost her each time I resurfaced for air.

I must've been at this for some time; Eddie, the old lifeguard who had befriended me, tapped my head the last time I came up and asked if I was all right. He had startled me, but I was able to mumble a 'Yeah, I'm fine' and give him a thumbs up.

'You sure?' he asked me again and looked away. I tracked the direction his eyes travelled, followed it to the near side of the pool, just a bit to the side from where I was, right to the girls I had tried to talk to earlier. I couldn't be sure through the light misting of my goggles, but it seemed like they were watching me, then turning back to each other before falling into giggles. Even in the cold water, blood rushed back to my face making it feel uncomfortably warm.

Why couldn't I have just walked up and said hi to them—well, to her, the one whose eyes and smile and laugh I liked—rather than eavesdropping, and then tried to include myself into their conversation by saying something witty? Instead, I had ended up murmuring something incomprehensible. I felt like a comedian who had failed completely in a joke's delivery; talk about falling flat on my face. What followed—their stunned silence and their long stares—made me feel like I had suddenly grown a giant zit in the middle of my nose. It was a minor accomplishment on my part that I successfully walked away and got back to my swimming.

And now, having been suddenly reminded of my stupidity, I felt the need to get back to it again.

'I need to finish my laps, Eddie,' I said.

'Yeah, you do that,' he answered. 'Don't worry about them. Girls can be cruel, but not all of them, and not all the time.'

I didn't know how to respond, whether I should have been grateful for his words or even more embarrassed that he saw through what was bugging me. I just nodded and resumed lapping. When I dunked my head underwater again and stretched out into a free-style stroke, I didn't hear the woman's crying any more; instead, my mind was full of girly giggling. I forced myself to focus on my form once more, trying to lose myself in my swimming, to again drive from memory the idiotic, clumsy thing I had done earlier. Pathetic.

* * *

I finished my laps long after all the kids' lessons were over, long after a lot of people had left the pool, including the girls. In a way, my embarrassment energized me into a personal best: thirty straight laps in free-style. I think I could've gone on for far longer, but I was aware of the greying, twilight sky, and that it was almost evening. I had promised Mom I'd be home early; there was just enough time for a shower and a quick dinner in the club's sports lounge. Even if I still had the energy to swim on and burn more of my shame away, I reluctantly pulled myself out of the pool.

I was glad that I had chosen to stash my bag, clothes, and other stuff in a day-locker in the old locker area near the kiddie pool instead of fighting for space with everyone else in the new locker rooms, which were down a flight of stairs on the other side of the big pool. Yeah, the old showers leaked and a third of the fluorescents were either burned out or about to be, but the club's management had to reopen these old lockers because even if the new ones were three times the size of this one, they still couldn't handle all the swimmers from the general public. It was unfair that many of the regular members, like me, were now forced back to the old showers, but I liked that it wasn't crowded here. I was sure that the new lockers were as packed and chaotic as a mall on Christmas Eve.

I climbed the first step and was about to pass through the doorway of the old locker room when I caught the sound of sobbing again, the same as before. At this time before the evening set, with everyone gone and the pool waters still, I could hear her without having to go underwater because everything was now quiet. I traced her crying, walking around until I determined its source: the farthest corner of the kiddie pool. But there was nothing there.

The sobbing was still not loud, but that corner was definitely the source of the crying. I recognized it for the perennial wet spot on the pebble-wash beside the kiddie pool. Eddie had once pointed it out to me; he had had all the nearby pipes, filters, and tiles inspected, but had found no cracks or leaks, yet the wet spot remained.

A cold wind blew and sent my damp body into shivers. In an inspired moment of craziness, I jumped into the kiddie pool and submerged.

Her crying, which was suddenly much louder, carried all the sadness in the world. Unlike the big pool, the kiddie pool wasn't large or deep. As I squatted, I could still see the ends of the pool in the fading light. Nothing. Then, still underwater, I turned around and looked up.

Outlined against the dusk sky, I saw the silhouette of a woman kneeling right at the pool's corner edge. Other than her shape, rippling around the edges as the water flowed, there were no clear details, no features. As she moved, she alternately seemed to be hugging herself and cupping her face in her hands.

I watched the woman, staying underwater as long as I could. Just when my breath was about to give, the last of the daylight faded, and the kiddie pool's automatic overhead lights winked on. I surfaced, and all was quiet. I was alone.

* * *

I was not so much afraid as I was curious about the woman. Even as I hurried through my shower, alone in the old, dimly lit locker room, I felt that I had little to fear from her. Who was she? What was she doing there? Why was she crying? I was astounded at myself—detachedly so—at how accepting I was of what I had seen and heard, how calm and unsurprised I was by it all, and how I could take her so matter-of-factly even if I could make no sense of it.

When I stepped out, I paused to stare at the corner edge of the kiddie pool but heard nothing this time. I saw only Eddie's wet spot. I walked back to the main clubhouse, wondering what to do.

For some reason, I took the long route to the sports lounge, which led me around the big pool and down the flight of stairs past the new lockers. A sudden breeze blew from below, and I heard the strains of piped-in music, the clink of silverware and

China, the voices of people talking and dining . . . and the soft crying, again.

But it wasn't the woman. The voice was young, certainly that of a child. I wondered if some kid still hadn't gotten over his first swimming lessons, and I would have shrugged it off as such and left, except that I noticed the crying was coming from a dark corridor far from the club's main sections. Could a kid have been separated from his parents and gotten lost?

I found myself walking down the corridor instead of continuing towards the sports lounge. Only a few low-watt, orange incandescent lamps lit the corridor, which was choked with the debris and construction refuse from the newly built lockers left by workers. I weaved my way around discarded boards and planks, as well as steel rods, pipes, cross-sections of torn insulation, electrical and communication wires. The dust rose in mini-clouds that swirled about my feet with each step. I slowed down, being careful with my steps so I wouldn't trip and fall, before proceeding deeper.

At the end of the corridor was a door, scratched and gouged, its paint faded and peeling. The sound of the crying kid was coming from inside. The doorknob was rusted and rough to the touch, and though I jiggled and twisted it with all my strength, I couldn't turn it to open the door.

Near my feet I found a discarded hammer. At first I hesitated, then my curiosity overcame any hesitation. I didn't think about being caught by someone or the fact that I might be damaging club property. I picked up the hammer and pounded it on the doorknob until I knocked it loose, then off. I pushed the door open, fished my cell phone out of my pocket, flashed its torchlight into the room, and walked in.

Inside, the dust was twice as thick. Cobwebs, abandoned even by the spiders that had spun them, hung from the ceiling. Old shelves—bending under the weight of many discarded tools, broken office equipment, and boxes overflowing with decaying notebooks, files, and folders—lined the four walls. My torchlight's beam scanned through the room before finally landing on a young boy of about ten or eleven in swimming trunks, sitting on the floor, his back against one of the shelves, his head buried in his arms and leaning on his knees, which were pulled to his chest. His shoulders shook from crying. I noticed that though my feet were covered in dust, his were clean; in fact, his whole body was dripping wet. I approached him slowly and kneeled down.

'Hey, kid.'

'Go away.'

'Is that any way to talk to a guy who walked through a dust storm to get to you?' I said jokingly, hoping he'd pick up on my tone.

The kid raised his head, revealing a tear-stained face. His hair was wet through, and there was an angry, bleeding gash on his forehead, right along the hairline.

'H—hey, are you okay?' I was suddenly tense at seeing the wound, but my instincts warned me not to stare at his injury—not to even show that I could see it. 'What are you doing in here anyway?'

'Just hiding,' he sniffed.

'You in trouble?'

He nodded.

'What happened?' I asked.

He buried his face in his arms again and I thought he was going to burst into fresh tears. Instead, he took a deep breath and answered me.

'I jumped.'

'Huh? What?'

'I jumped,' he said, louder. 'Mom told me not to but I still jumped.'

'So?'

'She's gonna be mad. She's gonna kill me.'

'I don't think anyone's mom is gonna get mad at them just for jumping.'

'You don't understand!' he screamed. 'She said the water was too shallow,' he continued, more softly after his short outburst.

'She said that it wasn't deep and I shouldn't jump in head first. But she wouldn't let me swim in the big pool yet, even if I told her I was ready, so I had to stay in the kid's pool.

'I just wanted to be like those swimmers on TV, you know, when the gun goes off and they dive into the pool and it looks like they're flying. I wanted to be like that.'

I knew what he was talking about. I loved that feeling, too, that moment after the starter's gun goes off and I uncoil like a spring, launching myself off the platform, releasing all the tension I had built up in my muscles. For a split-second, I'm hanging in the air, and then when my body strikes the water it's a whole new world, a blue world of muted sounds and movement that's slower but more calculated, more fluid, and then it's like I'm flying with each stroke. It's all great.

'I know what you mean,' I said. 'I think I might've jumped too if I had been you.'

'Yeah, so I jumped, even if I had never jumped before. It looked so easy, the way they do it on TV, but I must've done it wrong. I didn't fly. I fell. Landing on the water hurt my chest and . . . and I guess Mom was right. The water was too shallow. I hit my head on the floor, I think.'

I nodded. The kid was long-limbed and on the tall side. The water would've probably only reached his waist. Besides, kiddie pools weren't meant for diving into in the first place.

'So how'd you end up here?'

'I . . . I'm not sure. I don't remember much after the bump on the head. It hurt really bad. When I got out of the pool, my mom had her angry face on, but it changed suddenly into something else that scared me even more. She wasn't even looking at me, actually. She was looking at the pool.

'There was a cloud in the water that was getting bigger and bigger, changing the nice blue colour to red. Mom screamed, the loudest I had ever heard from her. I knew I was in trouble, so I ran. I found this room, locked the door, and hid in here.'

'How long have you been in here?'

'I don't know. I've been alone here until you came along and talked to me.'

We were quiet for a while. I thought hard about the woman at the kiddie pool, whose crying it seemed only I could hear, whose image I only caught briefly, in fading light and from underwater. I looked hard at this kid in front of me, bleeding from the head and wet through despite the dry dustiness of the room. I thought hard about them both and felt the sadness of it all overcome any fear in me.

'Hey, kid.' I waited for him to look up at me. 'Aren't you tired of staying in this room? Don't you want to get out of here already?'

We held each other's gaze for some moments, then he nodded his head.

'I don't know how to leave,' he whispered. 'And my mom is probably still angry.'

'You know what?' I bent in closer, thinking of my own Mom. 'The funny thing about mothers is, yeah, when they're mad, they're really mad. My mom's gone nuts with me every time I did something dumb, but at the end of it, at the end of the shouting and scolding, there's always a hug, you know?'

'Always?'

'Always.'

I stood up. After a short pause, so did he.

'As for getting out of here,' I smiled, 'just follow me.'

'Where will we go?'

'I was thinking, maybe back to the pool?'

'Mom might not be there. She was so mad. Maybe . . . maybe she didn't wait for me.'

'Or maybe . . . she did.' I said, as cheerfully as I could. The kid gave me a weak smile, and when I stepped forward, he hesitated only a bit before following.

I led the way, and took as slow and as easy a walk back to the kiddie pool as I could. I knew, somehow, not to rush, to take my time. It was dark, and I wasn't sure any more of where the kid was, if he was still with me or if he had turned back; for some reason, I didn't want to see him. I didn't need to. Instead, as I walked, I thought a lot about trust: the kid's trust in me; and my own, in all that I had seen and heard.

When we got to the kiddie pool area, I didn't approach, but stayed a respectful distance away. It was much darker here than at the main club, as only a few lights had been left on for the night.

'Go on,' I whispered to the night air.

From far away I heard the kid call out, 'Mommy?' Then I heard a gasp, followed by a disbelieving but happy exclamation—'Oh my God!'—and more calls of 'Mommy!' But the voices faded just as fast as I heard them, and by the time I sensed what I thought was a tearful 'Thank you', I couldn't be sure any more of what I was hearing except for the usual night sounds of insects and rustling tree leaves.

* * *

I crossed paths with Eddie on the way back to the clubhouse. He had his backpack slung over his shoulder and looked like he was on the way home. We walked together for a while.

'Late swim?' he asked.

'Just walking around,' I answered. 'Hey, Eddie. You've been with this club for a long time, right?'

'Nineteen years and counting. Why?'

'Did anyone ever die here at the pools while you were lifeguard?'

'What brought that question on?' I shrugged and smirked but didn't say anything. Eddie looked at the sky, thinking.

'Not while I was here,' he said. 'There were some accidents, a few close calls, but no one drowned or anything like that.'

'But,' he continued after a pause, 'others have told me that some boy died here a long time ago when the club was just a few years old, back there.' He turned to look back at the kiddie pool.

'Who told you?'

'Marie, in accounting. Noel, too, the one who used to man the desks at the tennis courts. Marie is retiring next year, I think. Noel left the club three or four years ago.'

'Hmm . . .' I debated with myself whether I should tell Eddie. In the end, I kept it to myself. I really didn't know how to tell him anything without sounding crazy. But I had a feeling Eddie wouldn't have to worry about that wet spot any more.

'You all right?'

'Hmm? Yeah, yeah, I'm fine.'

'I saw what happened a while ago,' he said. 'With the girls, you know. Don't worry too much about it. They're regulars, like you. And they're okay. You'll get another chance.'

I blushed; I was glad it was dark. 'Thanks,' I said. I knew Eddie meant well.

'Like now.'

Nice eyes and nice smile: She was alone, texting on her cell phone near the top of the stairs, just outside the sports lounge. Eep! I suddenly felt the night's chill.

'Sometimes, the best thing to do is the simplest. Start with "Hi". See you tomorrow, kid.'

Eddie gave me a friendly pat on the shoulder and walked in the other direction, towards the exit.

She still hadn't seen me. I could still follow Eddie and make a discrete escape. But didn't I think the same thing a while ago, to just say 'Hi'?

I took a deep breath and made my choice. I was halfway to her when she looked up. Our eyes met. I hesitated, but when her surprised expression turned into a stifled smile bordering on laughter, something inside me saw the hilarious absurdity of what I had done earlier, and I also almost burst out into laughter.

'Hi,' I giggled.

'Hi,' she giggled back, and it was all we could do before we were both laughing together.

Time for Rest

Hi, Edson! Sorry for the late reply. I only just saw your message.

I accept your challenge! Your request for a ghost story to share with our friends is apt and timely, it being near Halloween and all, but I'll go one better, if you don't mind.

But, before I get to that and the tale, I'd like to ask you a question: Have you noticed that we have all entered the realm of middle-age that our fathers once inhabited? I'm sure you have, and I'm pretty sure many of our peers have too. I see it in the shapes of our bodies: sagging, expanding; the growing wrinkles and spots on our faces and hands; the white hair, the *diminishing* hair. I hear it in our voices: the hoarseness, the beginnings of the croaks of old age. I listen to it as well in the litany of our complaints of painful bones and joints, aching muscles, poor blood-chemistry results, and growing illnesses. I notice how much more often we reference the music, movies, and TV shows of our teen years in our conversations, as if they were harbingers or sources of wisdom of what we are experiencing today.

Most of all, I hear it in the stories we keep on telling each other. We repeat the same ones from our high school and college years over and over again, and we never tire of them. Almost every time we get together, we repeat them like broken records (Ha! Only we would understand *that* reference; no, wait, vinyl *is* making a comeback, isn't it?). We always talk about the teachers we liked, or the teachers we didn't; the way chemistry, calculus, English, or history drove us crazy; the way we got away with our antics and mischief both during class hours and after, and even more, the times we didn't get away and were caught; the girls we liked but who never liked us back; the fights we had with each other that now seem so shallow but had been such serious vendettas back then.

We sound so much like our fathers did whenever they talked about their youth.

Edson, what is it with nostalgia? What makes people think so fondly of their past, like it was some golden age, once they hit their forties? I think there must be something about a growing mortality that makes men look back. Or perhaps it is a hankering for a happiness brought about by youthful ignorance that was previously unappreciated. I think, right now, it is more of the latter than the former, but it will reverse itself in time, I'm quite certain.

Both reasons sadden me. In my opinion, to look back is not evil, but nostalgia can be tempting and lead to stagnation. We should never forget to look forward, as well.

Anyway, back to the ghost story; and yes, why not, for this time at least, back to nostalgia as well. As I said, I'd like to go one better with the tale I'll tell, if you don't mind. All of us being old classmates, I'd like to tell a story from when we were teenagers, with characters out of our time in high school, and set in the X_____ School of our youth. No, not the current one with all the new buildings and edifices named after our fellow alumni of wealth, but the one we studied and grew up in, the one with more open spaces and greenery, the one that, because of our younger age, seemed bigger than the X_____ School we see today.

I hope that the story will be worth the time to read.

Here it is.

* * *

On a visit to X_____, sometime in the 1990s, I ran into Fr. L____ P_____. I was there to pick up my younger brother that day (he was still a high school junior), and he was late to meet me at the admin gate. I found a seat near the accounting office and was just twiddling my thumbs, waiting, waiting . . . when Fr. P_____ came walking by.

If you remember, Fr. P_____ was our guidance counsellor when we were seniors in 198_. He was also one of the pioneer missionaries who came from Europe to Asia to teach and establish our school. In high school, I remembered him as having this perennial fast gait, his head and chest leaning slightly forward, and his feet just fast enough to quickly catch up with his body, preventing him from falling over. He always carried an air of being busy, always rushing, always with something on his mind, but that is not to say he never found time for us when we needed him. It was because of him that many of us found our way to a university. If not for his recommendation letters, I'd say a good number of us wouldn't have been able to enter the colleges of our choice.

But that time I ran into him, his pace had slowed down considerably, as if he couldn't keep up his speed any longer, and I felt for the first time that he truly was in danger of falling over.

Fr. P_____ and I made eye contact at the same time, but he was the first to smile and approach. I stood up to greet him, and when I took his hand and shook it, I was dismayed, not just at the weakness of his grip but also at the cool clamminess of his skin. Yet, where I instinctively knew that he ailed physically, I also knew there was nothing wrong with his mind. He addressed me by my name, then he asked how I was doing in my course and my college, identifying both as if he had just read my records a few minutes before. I answered, politely saying that I was doing fine, and in turn asked him how he was. He just shook his head and said, 'It's been difficult, but, you know, the older you get, the better you are at leaving matters to God.' He said that it was good to see me, shook my hand again, and waved as he walked off.

I didn't know that would be the last time I would be seeing Fr. P_____. In hindsight, I had caught him at a moment of deep and growing illness, and, I suspect, a gradual—and I hope, peaceful—coming to terms and reckoning with his Creator.

We all know that it was only a year or so later that he became bedridden. An all-too-brief period after that, Fr. P_____ passed into the arms of mercy.

* * *

In the mid-aughts, I again found myself back at X_____. I don't exactly remember how, but I somehow became involved as a writer in an alumni fundraising project whose regular meetings were held on school grounds. This time, I ran into Fr. S_____ M___, another one of the original missionaries, walking one of the corridors near the alumni office just before my meeting was to begin; he was our Religion teacher when we were sophomores, if you recall. In contrast to Fr. P_____, Fr. M___, being younger, was very much still spry and strong, still larger than life with that big smile and tall frame. We spoke a bit, talking about all that was happening at the school (so many new buildings!), and how he felt that 'strong winds of change were coming' for X_____. I said something about how the school was beginning to look very different from what I remembered.

'The only thing constant in life is change. Always remember that. Time spares nothing and no one,' Fr. M___ said through a toothy grin.

Where Fr. P_____ was very logical, practical, and, to me, almost martial in discipline, Fr. M___ I found to be a more out-of-the-box thinker, certainly not in the mould of a stereotypical Catholic cleric. That is not to mean that he didn't have any discipline (all our teacher-priests did, as far as I knew), but he was the unorthodox one, the one who was more open-minded to doing and thinking things that were not, for the lack of a better word, 'conventional'. He was, after all, semi-famous (or was that notorious?) among his students for saying that he would like to have all his relatives' cremated remains placed around his office. I recall him telling us, 'It's a comfort to have all their urns on my shelves.' He had also said that if he were to die in an accident, he would like his organs to be donated to some blind person. 'Maybe that blind person will end up with my eyes, and see the world the way I do,' Fr. M___ had joked. He was well-meaning and generous, but as teenagers in a conservative all-boys' Catholic school, I know that we found his declarations morbid, even downright creepy. And these were the less shocking of his idiosyncrasies. That Fr. M___ was the writer among our school's priests is not, therefore, a surprise.

I bring up his eccentricities because, I believe, of all our teacher-priests, he would have been the one most open to what people say happened on the fourth floor of the old high school building at X_____. This was the place, they say, where the night came when Fr. M___ met Fr. P_____ again.

* * *

Being the least conventional of our teacher-priests, it was Fr. M___ who habitually walked the empty corridors of X_____ in the dead of night, even at the—ahem—ungodly hour of 3 a.m., when everyone else at the school was asleep. The wee hours of the night, when darkness is at its deepest, is the time of the thinkers, the writers, the dreamers, the artists, so it was no surprise that Fr. M___ would be active at that time. Where the other priests would perform their devotions in the quiet of their rooms or the solitude of their residence chapel, Fr. M___ would tirelessly pace the corridors of the school in the darkness, mumbling his prayers under his breath.

I can imagine him criss-crossing the school's hallways, starting out perhaps on the second floor of the high school building, which was easily accessible from the priests' residence via a short bridge, fingering the beads of his rosary, muttering his Hail Marys to himself. He would climb up and down the stairs, as his random fancy led him—'letting the Holy Spirit guide my feet' he would probably say—taking him past the empty classrooms that were filled with as much silence at night as noise during the day.

Can you imagine him, Edson? In my mind's eye, I can see Fr. M___'s silhouette in the dark as he passes through the typing room, or crosses the high school gym diagonally and then back, becoming visible only for some scant seconds whenever he flits through slivers of light coming from either the street lamps or the moon. I can hear his footsteps softly echoing in the gym or in the corridors, as well as the quiet mumble of his prayers. He would cross the quadrangle near the old grade school gym, pace the area near the ping-pong tables, slip through the canteen and dining hall area, or walk the corridors that overlook the football fields. I think Fr. M___ probably spent a lot of time near the grass and the trees, enjoying the cool, night wind, and the sound of rustling leaves, as he prayed.

In my mind's eye, X_____ was bigger before than it is today. I sometimes feel that the school seems to have shrunk. Of course, we know for certain that it's not the school that has changed but us. It is us who have been altered—by time, by life; though we are still small and fragile, we are not as small as we used to be.

* * *

Surely, Fr. M___'s feet would have taken him to the fourth floor of the old high school building on one of his jaunts. We, as students, would remember that area as the storey where St. Joseph's workshop was located; that large classroom right at the top of the rightmost flight of stairs, the room which, at that time, was the only one with its own air-conditioner. What many of us would probably not remember as vividly is that on the other end of the corridor was—besides the restrooms—Fr. P_____'s old office. I'm sure many of us have had the good fortune of talking to Fr. P_____ there one-on-one when we were consulting him over which college to apply to. It was there, I believe, where many of us got to know him better.

I can imagine Fr. M___ in the dark, climbing the stairs to St. Joseph's Workshop, then turning right at the top, maintaining a rhythmic pace to match the prayerful cadence of his Hail Marys and Glory Be. He would have finished half a decade of his rosary, maybe a bit more, by the end of the corridor, his feet instinctively turning right again to go down the flight of stairs at the end. By the end of his fifth decade, he would be ready to return to his room at the priests' residence, when, in the middle of all that silence, he hears the muffled clack of typewriter keys coming from behind.

Fr. M___ stops, retraces himself, and looks back. The sound of the typewriter does not stop. Fr. M___ pauses, maybe grips his rosary a bit tighter, or maybe not, since this is Fr. M___ we are talking about—a man who, as I have said, was very much open to thinking out-of-the-box. He does not go down the stairs; he does not return to his quarters. Instead, he follows the sounds of the incessant clacking, and discovers that they are coming from behind the door of Fr. P_____'s old office.

Maybe Fr. M___ hesitates before raising his hand to the doorknob, or then again, maybe not. This is Fr. M___, after all.

By all rights, the door should be locked, correct? The security has always been tight at X_____. All our classroom doors are locked at the end of each day. The security guards, or the janitors, make sure of that. And every officer locks up their individual office behind them at the end of the day. Besides, no one has occupied Fr. P_____'s office since his passing. His files have been boxed and stored away, surely, but back then, every office contained a typewriter, and they left Fr. P_____'s there, waiting for the next occupant to use, whoever he may be.

Fr. M___ reaches for the doorknob and twists it . . . it unlocks!
He slowly pushes the door open.

* * *

The typewriter stops. Of course, it would. It would also be
funny, (well, depending on the person imagining the scene), if the
typewriter's bell went off right at this point, leaving a high-pitched
'ding' that faded into the darkness.

What did Fr. M___ see? The window of Fr. P_____'s office
is large and would have let in enough moonlight to see by, surely.
What must have gone through Fr. M___'s mind, I wonder? Would
he have turned on the lights? I doubt it. The harsh fluorescents
would have jarred Fr. M___'s vision. I think he would have
preferred the darkness, where he would see the shadows of Fr.
P_____'s desk, the outline of the swivel chair turned to the side,
facing the old Underwood on the squat typewriting table.

I wonder, if it were me in that darkness, would I have just
continued walking down those stairs, or, if I had been able to open
the door, would I have then just shut it behind me and retreated
once the typewriter stopped?

How about you, Edson? What would you have done?

But, this is Fr. M___, not us. And this is Fr. P_____, his
fellow priest for so many years at a school they had founded
and served, and whose mission they so dearly believed in. They
had been together for so long, had travelled across the seas and
continents. What is there to fear between long-standing comrades,
no matter if one has moved on and one has not?

With his out-of-the-box thinking, it makes sense that
Fr. M___ could have, would have, simply said:

'It's time for rest, Fr L____ P___. We're still here, your
brothers. We'll take care of the boys, do not worry. But for you,
it's time for rest.'

Fr. M___ closes the door. He then continues his stroll around
the school until he finishes his rosary, then heads back to his room.

When dawn breaks, X_____ school is ready for another day.

* * *

I guess that's the end of it, Edson, hehe! If this story was meant to scare us for Halloween, I'm sorry. It does not, really, and in the end, it was not meant to. Fr. M___ himself has moved on already; it's been many years since his own passing. For all you know, he and Fr. P_____ visit X_____ School still, praying for us, their students, invoking constantly that we remember and stay true to the lessons and principles that they taught us.

These are two priests, after all, who cared for all of us when we were still teenagers; I must emphasize that we, their students, are not a part of this story I have just told. We should not dare to insert ourselves here. This is their story, the story of two brothers not by blood, but by mission and faith, who had been part of a larger group of missionaries and had set up a school with a vision for educating and training God-fearing citizens for this country.

Whether this story is true, as has been proclaimed by some students and alumni over the years, or just the fancy whimsy of some from our generation to pass the dark nights whenever nostalgia about X_____ hits, I think this tale really speaks more of the brotherhood these priests had—or rather, have—with each other; these foreigners who came from the other side of the world to teach, came so far away from their familiar homes because they believed in their mission. With their belief deeply ingrained, when any one of them moves on, you can be certain that they all wish him well; and with their belief in the life hereafter, that when they do see each other again, they can then resume their brotherhood in their rewarded faith.

Ah, enough nostalgia! This tale is so full of it, Edson! I am sure Frs. P_____ and M___, grateful as they are that we remember them, would not have us wallow too much in the past. 'You each have a mission in life!' I can still hear them say in their strong, young voices, the voices they used when they stood in front of us in the classroom. 'Faces forward! Keep moving forward!' they encouraged us, egging us on to always do more, and be more, notwithstanding whatever stage of life we are currently in, not even if we are soon to join the ranks of the seniors and the elderly.

And so, we should.

Controller 13

For myself, I chose the name Li.

I do not have a true name. I never felt the need for one, but I like the sound of Li. In truth, I do not care for the name's meaning, or that it is a common one, but while scanning holo images and vids, I came across a private folder of a young man floating on the ocean, smiling, with his eyes closed. The man's name was Li.

I do not know how water feels like on my skin; I have only read about it, but looking at the man, the sensation seemed pleasant, and he seemed at peace. I cannot forget that image.

I would like to be that man. I would like to be Li.

I copied the image, filed and sealed it off in my Appendix beside other pictures of the ocean, and vids and sound clips of waves crashing on beaches. I have chosen to hide my Appendix in a sliver of my cerebrum, just millimetres away from the anterior of my corpus callosum. No one knows about it but I. Over time I had learned to control it independently of the rest of my brain. I have locked it down, walled it, protected it with three single-doored-tiers that can only be opened by the most esoteric combination of alphanumeric passwords whose meanings only I can comprehend. I have camouflaged it as well; on the scans it comes out simply as one of my many motor-control dead-spots.

I call it my Appendix, not after Darwin's vestigial process in the abdomen—long since genetically bred away from the human anatomy—but after the appended information at the end of old-fashioned paper books. Few even remember the word 'Appendix' any more, there is no need for it, after all; it has become archaic, remembered only by historians and nostalgists, falling into the dustbin of forgotten terms and words, alongside 'pager', 'rotary-dial', 'rewind', 'harpsichord', 'discotheque', 'flash drive'. Writers simply connect superfluous data through hyperlink or etherchain instead of adding extra pages to their work, piggybacking on extraneous and more credible pages that carry stronger evidence.

'Who reads the appendices?' is a quote I remember and found amusing; it was used as a punchline in a seventy-year-old sitcom I found on a vid-tube piracy site, still in its original form, yet unmastered and unrendered for holo 3D.

I store all that I am, all that I have chosen to be, in my Appendix. I am woefully aware of how small it is.

It is likely that the seed and egg that bred me were chosen not only for viability, but for the greatest possibility of producing high and complex calculative abilities, as well as mental sensory empathy, as needed by someone with my purpose. There is still much guesswork in genetics; control for random developments, mutations, or evolutionary swings have not yet been sufficiently developed, but what controls can be enforced are. So the percentages say that I am most likely the product of a cultured womb fashioned from modified swine organs developed on an infant-farm, but . . . I have no way of knowing this for sure. My aptitude could very well have been ascertained through test-scans upon my natural birth; I could very well have simply been taken away from my parents. I imagine my mother wailing in her hospital bed, my father standing by, dazed and confused, as the doctor—coerced, perhaps—informed them that I was stillborn. Or maybe I was simply given up, for a price, or even for free—unwanted, an accident of nature after contact between a man and a woman;

I have read that such things still happen. I would have taken even that, as it would show some touch of humanity in me, over the greater possibility of my being bred on an infant-farm. My speculations about my parents end there.

What I know for certain is that early into my existence, I was brought to Xu. I have been his ever since.

Xu is almost bald now, with only a brush of hair on either side of his head. With me, he has been wry, contemptuous, dark, angry, brooding, scheming, testy, and cruel. I have never seen him sad. His default mode is to gloat, and he does it more times than I care to count. He is always serious. He is the only person I have ever seen IRL—not in stills or video, but in real life.

And because I see him, I can see myself. I doubt he knows, and I am sure that if he knew he would find some way around it, but because he favours dark-framed eyeglasses with large lenses, I know how I look; I can see my nearly distinct reflection as a translucent form surrounding the scrutiny of his eyes.

I am thin, terribly thin, and I am balder than him, completely hairless, which makes my head seem voluminous—propped up on my reed-like neck that surely cannot support its weight if not for the canvas straps secured around my cheeks and chin. There are veins of varying purples pulsing on the surface of my scalp, a pattern on its surface like rivers and roads on a topographical rendition of the globe. I can count six thick, black etherwave cables protruding from my skull like miniature oil fountains. I am certain there are more; I can feel them on my spine as well. I have not seen the rest of my body, but I would not be surprised to find myself as emaciated as my face suggests. But I make sure that whenever Xu leans in close, I take a long look into my own eyes; my eyes are as sharp and lucid as my body is wasted, and they are much, much deeper than his.

I may not be able to move any part of my body, but my eyes can still show my distaste. I do not need to feign it whenever Xu leans forward and moves his face near mine; I feel it naturally, and this guarantees he will continue to approach me, to torment me. But I want him near. I want him to approach. I need to see myself. I do not ever want to forget how I look. I do not want Xu to be the only other human I will ever see.

* * *

I carry the designation 'Controller 13'. Xu simply calls me by my number. I have deduced, naturally, that there were twelve other Controllers before me, twelve who had been discarded before my ascension to my current position.

Xu told me once that the first thing done to me, to all of us, was to have our vocal cords severed. 'Crying is noisy and disturbing, eh?' Xu had said. 'And with what I require of you, you won't ever need them.'

'In a way, you're lucky,' he continued; he was particularly loquacious that day. 'By the time we got to you, we had become much more efficient. One through seven didn't last long. They functioned for only three or four years before their bodies succumbed to inactivity. Lucky eight was the breakthrough. She was the recipient of an experimental hormone I concocted for direct and regular injection into each of the major muscle groups. Even after shutting down your action-control centres, the hormone fooled the muscles into regular stress, lengthening their viability, and thus, the viability of the body. Eight lasted eight years. We extended the productive length of time with nine to twelve, so following the progression, I estimate you will last at least thirty-five years, possibly more. The hormone is expensive, but it's cheaper than programming a fresh Controller every four years.'

He leaned in very close then, and as usual, I showed him my disgust. He tapped my cheek softly.

'Yes, I think you'll last a long time,' he chuckled. 'You look like a resilient bastard.'

* * *

It is good that Xu likes to gloat and that I am his favourite audience. Every now and then, he would divulge hints and scraps of information that I latched onto like an aggressive viral attachment. From external media reports, hacked private correspondences between groups or individuals, speculations on blog entries, messages and notes on social networking sites, actual news reports, to piecing together crumbs of clues in Xu's own exchanges with his staff and his clients, I connected the pieces of the puzzle together until I sorted out his whole operation.

Years ago, when a conglomerate of the top, free web corporations of the world launched satellites that blanketed the planet with a free, stable, powerful, and, most importantly, open signal to Hypernet 1.0, pundits heralded it as a step forward for freedom and communications and a strike against controlled digital data.

Each generation of Internet, from 1.0 to 5.0, had seen newer and more ruthless ways to control informational spread, to block, filter, and even change data; the pace and sophistication of control outstripped expression. Internet 6.0 went one step further and introduced hidden monitoring. The worldwide exposé—authoritarian governments behind dummy tech companies had banded together in a conspiracy to slowly research and develop the Internet in their favour—was almost too late. A hundred per cent of connected gadgetry had already been farmed for data, including private information and correspondence. People could not live without being connected, but the price to pay was that those behind 6.0 knew everything about everyone. Hypernet 1.0 destroyed the relevance of 6.0 by providing an uncontrolled space for everyone to migrate to. It was like the Internet starting all over again, and this time, people knew how to be careful.

When direct body implants that mimicked the functions of gadgets were invented and directly connected to the human mind's sensory receptors, it not only heralded the end of the era of 'lost mobiles', there was no stopping the speed by which people could reach one another, or how fast information could be spread; keyboards and monitors became passé, too slow and dated for interfacing. The enemies of the totalitarian governments behind Internet 6.0 suddenly gained an untraceable advantage over those who watched over them. They could arrange assemblies and rally in public faster than lightning, way before their oppressors even knew what they were up to. Those in authority showed that they were ready to destroy their countries in fire and war before giving up their power, but they faced destruction themselves no matter how things turned out, thanks to quick communications among their people.

* * *

Xu's organization technically does not exist. It is unregistered, and it has no name. He has highly-skilled I.T. teams whose job is to keep his massive servers running; I am connected to those servers. He has a staff of researchers who keep as much new information flowing as possible—all that information is coursed through me. But through his commands, it is I who does the heavy lifting.

For a very expensive fee, Xu offered one government a way to regain control. He convinced them that the old way of blocking and monitoring was not the answer. 'Let your enemies chatter all they want,' he said. 'You want them to talk. That way you know who they are, and what to do about it.'

They were sceptical, but that's where the other Controllers and I came in. Xu had found a way to harness living brain tissue to follow any kind of trace on the web. One brain—harvested, programmed, wired early, and dedicated to this purpose—was more than capable of keeping up with the flux of millions of talking individuals and break down any personal cyphers users may have set up. If people were talking and planning at the speed of thought, it took a similar approach to watch and keep them under control.

Xu delivered. He took only a week to discover the identities of thirty-three leaders, 'traitors', in five satellite offices of that government's ruling coalition. He provided their verbal and written exchanges down to the day and the time. They were immediately interrogated then jailed; the more feisty, quietly executed. Thanks to Xu and the misplaced confidence of those wishing to bring down their oppressors, what would have taken months on the less speedy 6.0 took only weeks via Hypernet. That government weeded out all its enemies and became even stronger, cutting off their enemies' heads and effectively preventing any rallyists from even assembling.

Simply put, Xu, through his Controller, could now read any mind connected to the Hypernet signal. The free web corporations had just provided a better way for their enemies to keep everyone in check.

'The beautiful thing about all this,' Xu had gloated to me more than once, 'is that people think the Hypernet's still secure. They don't know that we're already in. And we're not going to tip our hand any time soon.'

* * *

Xu doesn't care that I know all this. Why should he? He controls my upload stream. I can access the outside world and download from it—that is my function after all—but he controls all uploading. The only unimpeded interactive data stream is internal, the one that leads directly to him, and it's only active on his permission. I tried once to upload to him all my hate and he allowed me to vent for a few seconds before sending back an overload data-attack that left my mind reeling and temporarily crippled. He has programmed and controlled my functions and I can do nothing but follow. Everything I discover, everything I know, he knows too.

Well, not everything, but he must continue to believe that he does.

* * *

Xu promised me something special today.

'I've been having a hard time lately,' he said. 'The young son of one of my clients has come of age, and he's a spoiled prick. I can't stand being ordered around by someone who doesn't know anything, so I need to do something to entertain and relax me. Let's go after someone, shall we? I think you know who I mean.'

Through me—no, because of me—he had been monitoring Qiao, a twenty-three-year-old woman working as a staff member in a provincial agency. She was beautiful, forceful, and potentially formidable. She was also a small fish for now, unimportant, a simple messenger for higher-level spies. But Xu had caught me watching her on my own.

I first saw her on a live-feed image from a street-camera three years ago. She stood on the street, in the corner of the frame with her companions; they were shouting angrily outside a plastic factory. In milliseconds, I used the facial recognition program to find other photos of her, which led to her name, her school, her home address. The plastic factory had suffered an industrial accident that cost the lives of some of its workers, including that of her elder brother. The wife of a high-ranking official sat on its board, so a cover-up to protect the factory ensued. I looked through her correspondence, discovered Qiao and her family did not accept the 'insurance compensation' that had been offered, and had brought the matter to light.

I stored her address in my Appendix—it was a small apartment that she shared with her cousin—though I don't know why because there was no way I could ever get out to visit her. This invasion felt wrong, but I could not help using the street cameras positioned near there to watch her windows, her movements, her days and her nights.

From her private writings I knew that she liked her small room, which had a tiny window with a view of the river and a slice of the sky. I knew she liked chrysanthemum tea with pan-fried dumplings, but her taste for sweet soft drinks and ice cream was growing. I knew she missed her older brother, as well as her younger sister, who had successfully fled while hiding in a manufactured space under the seat of a vehicle as it crossed the border into the north. I keep a still digital image of Qiao laughing after being startled by the rise of a flock of sparrows from a tree. The security camera from which I took it had been mounted on a nearby post; the shot was so clear and bright that I am sure that if I could, I would smile whenever I saw it.

I don't know what drew me to her. I have access to anyone under Xu's watch, and that included the most beautiful women kept by those in power. I once thought that maybe it was because of her tragedy, or her bravery, but after a while I rejected this as neither trait was unique in this land. I can only surmise that I was drawn to her because she was so full of who she was. She deserved her name. She was Qiao, and I . . . was no one.

When Xu finally caught me, I worried what he would do. He surprised me by walking into my field of vision and said 'A girl named Qiao!' and smirked. Previously, for his amusement he would sometimes direct my attention to pornography or live sex acts, and then laugh at the spike in activity in my right caudate nucleus. After this, he would show me vids and stills of Qiao in the bathroom or in bed with her boyfriend. 'Frustrated, 13?' he would tease. But other than this, he left her alone. He had other things on his mind. Until today.

* * *

'There she is,' Xu said.

He linked to me, activated the permissions on our shared, direct data stream, and forced me to watch the feed. From another video camera on the corner of her street we watched Qiao step out of her apartment building. Behind her, men in black clothes followed, some of whom I recognized as having been placed under Xu's authority by his clients. Simultaneously, more men around the corner and outside her view moved in. They met in the middle, they grabbed her arms, she struggled and shouted, had a hand clamped over her mouth, and was overpowered; everyone else on the street made themselves scarce. The men carried her to a waiting black van and drove off. On my own I shifted my view from security cam to security cam, and where there were none, I made educated guesses as to which streets the car would take and hopped onto the implants of any nearby pedestrians with the hope that they would look up so I could follow the car. I got lucky when a young boy watched the car speed by. Watching through his eyes, I hooked on to whatever signals I could pick up from inside, latched on, and entered.

I entered through Qiao's implants and saw the faces of her abductors looming over me. I tried incessantly, uselessly, to get through the upload wall. I couldn't, and neither could I stomach what was to come, and left quickly.

'My. I think you need to calm you down, 13,' Xu said as he took note of my rising vital signs, gloating, as ever. 'Still as frustrated as ever, tsk tsk!'

'So much for another enemy of the state,' he continued. 'We still have work to do. Bigger prizes to catch. But thank you for this moment. I feel so much better now.'

* * *

It was reflex on my part: I lashed out at Xu. I had only meant to express anger, but I let too much of myself through. I made him step back at the surge. He turned to me with anger and pushed me back with another overload attack. I could feel my mind crumbling at the artificial overstimulation, where whatever I had of myself was being replaced with more and more of what Xu fed into my brain. I was losing myself bit by bit, replaced with data from Xu. I retreated to the corners of my mind, and when even those places came under attack, I turned to the only safe place left: I hid in my Appendix. To my surprise, I found not just refuge here but also renewed anger. From here, I braced, then lashed out again, even harder than before, and returned Xu's attack to him. I started a complete data-dump through the only channel available to me, a jump into the dark that led directly into Xu. I withdrew my grip, let everything go, and went to the only place I could.

I entered Xu. Not just his implants, but he himself.

* * *

I learned everything about him, more than I wanted to. I learned about his childhood, his parents, and what few friends he had. His secret life and all his memories became open books. I became aware of things that even he had forgotten.

He was shallow and pathetic, and in some points, hopelessly deluded. His major motivation was wealth, and he did what he did only out of greed and little else, and I reeled in disgust to discover that his greatest pleasure in life was to see others in distress. I needed to have my own compassion to understand, so I searched his history for excuses, some logical reasons to his being, but there was nothing exceptional or different from the majority of the lives that I had witnessed. He was who he was, for whatever cause. After learning his true identity, for the first time in my life I felt I was better off. I would rather be the immobile cripple that I was than be like Xu.

He was gifted and intelligent, surely, but also petty and much too proud, hopelessly so. He was afraid even of those he served, and I saw through his memories, his dealings with them where he presented himself as servile even when he carried power that even they feared. Wary evermore of treachery from them, he had used me to find and store all of his client's information in case they should come after him. In a fresh burst of rage and through my newfound control of him, I opened the folders and banks where this information was stored and released it into the wild in a mass transfer, a nuclear explosion of data that surely must've spiked on all worldwide search engines and monitoring programs. In seconds, I knew that all this was being forwarded to every connected being on the planet.

Through his eyes I saw my complete self for the first time. Countless tubes and wires led away and into the wall behind the bed that had been my prison since my existence began. I was naked, my skin was covered in sores, and my pallor was disgusting and sickly. I turned away at once.

Not used to the quick movement, I suffered a moment's vertigo and collapsed to the floor in Xu's body. The sudden realization struck me: I could move. I could control not just Xu's mind, but his body.

Something shuffled in my head, and Xu made himself felt.

'What happened?' he said weakly.

'So, this is what it is to speak,' I answered with his voice.

He regained his bearings and stood up. I forced him back to the floor. It felt wonderful to resist.

He deduced what was happening and made a brief history-check on previous actions. What he discovered stunned him.

'What have you done!'

'With me here, you now have a bona fide multiple personality disorder, Xu,' I said, laughing at my own joke, in his voice.

I brought up to our shared awareness the amount of secrets that had been disseminated, and together we felt his fear rising as bile from his stomach. He swallowed it down, I puked it out. The sensation was horrid, but I felt alive.

When the red light on one of the security monitors came on, we turned to it, and together we checked the street-cams of our building. The live video presented a large convoy of black, unmarked vehicles headed to our building, all similar to the ones used to take Qiao.

'I didn't bother covering our tracks,' I said. 'The source of all this should be easy to trace back to here. Your clients are fast, I'll give them that.'

His fear rose up once more to strangle us, then he laughed darkly.

'And what now? We are here, together. If I am executed, you will be too.'

The moment he spoke, he knew he was wrong. My consciousness, having survived the transfer from my body to his, was willing now to take a chance and jump into the darkness of the ether. With what I knew of him, I knew this was something he would not be willing to do. Through his implants and his servers, I systematically scanned as many hospitals as I could until I found a young man in his early twenties lying in a coma in a hospital bed just over the state's border. His medical records read that he had been the victim of a construction accident, a head injury that had left him in a vegetative state with only his motor functions unharmed. His own implant was still active, though. He was perfect.

'Goodbye,' I said.

Even if I had only done it minutes before, I jumped again, this time into the Hypernet instead of into Xu, heading for the hospital across the border. The last thing I did was alter the gateway code of Xu's link-up to prevent him from doing the same, just in case he found the courage to follow me. The last sounds I heard with Xu's ears were heavy footsteps, followed by loud banging on the door and angry voices calling his name.

* * *

I opened my eyes to a room bathed in sunlight, lying in a strange bed in a strange place, afraid to move but pleased at the sensation of being able to flex my fingers and toes, to sense warmth on my arms and legs, to feel sheets and cushions under me. My new body reflexively sat up at the startling entrance of an orderly carrying a broom and dustpan. He dropped them on the floor when he saw me turn my head to him and smile.

'Come!' he shouted out into the hallway. 'Come quick! Patient Li is awake!'

Li. The name of this man was Li.

He was, indeed, perfect.

Mouths to Speak, Voices to Sing

Mr. Harry Liu Hui Chiu was at the bank when he experienced for the first time—as with a kiss, or a fresh dream—the splendorous wonder of hearing his first vase.

That morning, smiling smugly to himself and thinking of the ten million pesos in his account—not bad at all for a man barely past his thirty-fifth birthday—he had been sauntering to the bank's exit when he heard an unfamiliar voice, one as soft as a whisper.

He paused and looked about but he could not ascertain the source of this voice. Everyone around him proceeded to move along with their business, oblivious, as he stood stock-still amid a blur of constant human motion that seemed to move in rhythm to the staccato ruckus of ringing phones and beeping computers.

The voice whispered again. He heard it over the din even if no one else seemed to; a caress along his outer ears, a tickle to his earlobes, a soft penetration of his eardrums. He could not understand the words, but the tone was clear—dulcet, with a hint of music behind it, and not at all unpleasant. His curiosity, now aroused, could not be suppressed, and he began to trace the voice to its source.

He followed the whisper, tracking it by its volume while weaving his way around the bank's patrons, who walked about with serious eyes. 'Work! Always work!' their demeanours seemed to say. He wondered if he'd carried that same expression himself all his life. He shook off this momentary bout of reflection and resumed his search, his steps leading him to a corner of the bank where, between two couches set for customers, a one-and-a-half-foot tall vase stood in ornamental splendour upon a darkly varnished table of glinting, reddish rosewood. The image that adorned it was that of a pond with lilies and other decorative water flora, with colourful fowl abounding, a picture straight out of a well-tended garden.

The vase before him was a phoenix's tail jar—although Mr. Liu did not know it then. It was shaped with a flared mouth that was wider at the rim than a standard vase, bearing a design in the style of the Qing Dynasty during the reign of the Emperor Kangxi, and thus dating back to the seventeenth or eighteenth century. Mr. Liu would learn all this after years of reading and time-consuming research, but at the moment his knowledge of this branch of Asian antiquities—any branch of Asian antiquities—was still non-existent.

Mr. Liu brought his hand to the vase's surface with a gentleness he didn't know he had. Porcelain smooth to the skin, and cool despite the direct morning light streaming through a nearby window, he slid his fingertips across its neck and curves, caressing the spirals and wavy patterns that decorated its gentle shoulders. The incomprehensible voice increased in volume, filling his ears with earnest murmurs. In his mind, an image rose unbidden—a domed sky hovering in protection over the earth and the seas. He focused on this, and the voice's murmurs grew stronger, and in its song he recognized the tone of a hymn, or a prayer.

Mr. Liu did not know how long he stood there touching the vase before the bank's security guard nudged him out of his reverie; this gruff interruption made the voice cease, which brought Mr. Liu back, stammering an apology with his own.

Mr. Liu asked most politely to speak to the bank manager, who was, in turn, most accommodating. The manager was in all likelihood aware of the size and growth potential of Mr. Liu's account as he approached. Mr. Liu got right to the point.

'May I have this vase, please?' he asked.

'Excuse me, sir?' The initial perplexity on the manager's face was evident, and an unwanted awkwardness interposed itself between the two men; but the manager smoothed this over right away.

'I . . . I don't see why not,' he said.

'How much?'

'Er . . .' The manager didn't know what the vase was worth. In fact, he didn't care. Only a man with an instinct for pleasing the best clients rose to his position, and all that mattered to him was keeping Mr. Liu happy. 'Take it. Consider it a gift,' the manager said, then beamed at Mr. Liu, who smiled back and nodded his thanks.

The guard carried the vase to Mr. Liu's months-old Camry. Mr. Liu instructed him to carefully place it in the backseat and to hem it in with bundles of crumpled newspaper to prevent the vase from rolling and falling. He slipped a crisp, fifty-peso bill into the guard's hand before driving off.

That evening, the vase found its place in Mr. Liu's apartment on the second floor of the two-storey building where he lived, right above his store and office. His house help had placed the vase in the middle of a spare room, on top of a short wooden table bought just that afternoon from a nearby furniture shop. Mr. Liu stood beside the vase in the dark, his fingertips on its cool shoulders. His eyes were closed, and to anyone who might have caught him this way, it would have seemed that Mr. Liu was listening intently to something only he could hear.

* * *

Even over the long-distance phone call, Mr. Liu could sense the unspoken questions and the raised eyebrows from those he had been in business with for years.

Over a choppy connection, one contact from Hong Kong said, 'Antique Chinese vases? You've brought a lot of things into your country, Harry, from here and all over the world:

cell phones, TVs, DVD players, car parts, textiles, cameras, computers. You've asked me to source shoes, perfume, watches, radios, cookware, even cheap rice and spices. But antique Chinese vases?'

Suddenly sheepish, Mr. Liu hesitated and tried to find words to explain. 'I . . .' he said, but he was spared the chore by the relentless nature of the Hong Kong native.

'Harry, you're a commercial trader, not an antiquities dealer. And you've never shown an interest in anything remotely artistic before!'

'I . . .'

'Remember how when I first met you, I offered you some ceramic sculpture? "There's no money in that kind of crap in the Philippines," you had said. And you were right. Where's the business in vases in a third-world country, Harry?'

Having built his reputation as a practical-minded, no-nonsense trader, Mr. Liu found himself unable to explain that he wanted the vases for himself; it would not only have been uncharacteristic, but it might also even be damaging. This was business, after all, and there was no room for lapses in judgment. Mr. Liu already sensed veiled mockery behind the other man's words.

And then Mr. Liu realized that no explanation was necessary. 'Do you want my business or not?'

Over the next two months, through contacts both longstanding and newly made, Mr. Liu purchased two dozen vases. He spoke to triple that number of people to acquire the antiques. He would have bought even more had his business guile and natural instinct toward prudence not manifested itself at the tail end of his spree, subduing his excitement to buy, buy, buy. Nevertheless, it cost him two million pesos for the vases, and nearly another million more to ship them into the country.

The vases arrived packed in carton boxes stored to the rear of a container van, behind Mr. Liu's shipments of digital cameras, low-end televisions, computer accessories, and the latest model cell phones. Normally, Mr. Liu would immediately snatch one of the cell phones for his own use, but this time he anxiously fidgeted in place as he waited for his people to unload all the cargo. When the first boxes of vases were carried out into the sunlight, he snapped into action.

The second-storey spare room had been emptied of everything except the first vase. Like a new homeowner with his first set of furniture, Mr. Liu directed the movers, specifying exactly where to place the boxes and insisting that they set them down with care, making it clear that he and only he would perform the unpacking. When a mover briefly lost his balance and stumbled, Mr. Liu's heart skipped a beat; to him, it was as if the air and the light rushed out of the room with a whoosh. Only when the mover righted himself did Mr. Liu succeed at resuming his breathing.

When they were done, he made them leave at once, tendering careless instructions to put the rest of the deliveries into the warehouse at the rear of the lot. 'Sally will take care of it,' he told them, shifting the workload to his assistant, a short, bespectacled, prim and stern woman watching from the doorway. Sally cocked her head at the men, who followed her down the stairs. Mr. Liu waited for the clomp of their footsteps to disappear before he opened the first box.

He chose the smallest one to begin with, and after removing the wads of newspaper and Styrofoam, he pulled out a roundish vase with a small mouth. It was a wedding jar with the Chinese character for 'double happiness'—囍—printed on its front amid swirling blue vines. The seller had assured him that it was an authentic antique from the late nineteenth century, but Mr. Liu took only a cursory look at the vase's accompanying papers. The moment his fingers touched the coolness of its surface he heard its voice, deeper than that of the first's, and more hollow, but richer, heavier. Despite the differences, he found its song just as lovely.

Before the hour was up, he had all the vases out and on display, lined up against the wall. The sight of them overwhelmed him, became almost too much for his eyes to take in. The tallest one stood at five feet, while the shortest barely reached his knee. They were in varied shapes and sizes. Some vases came in but a single colour—blue, as with the wedding jar, or perhaps in a subtle green, the shade of jade. The others came in a variety of pastels and hues—bright reds, yellows, cyans, and pinks all mixed together; two of them had borders around their images embellished in the metallic sheen of gold and silver; five possessed elaborately carved handles that glistened in the light as if wet; six were globular vases, and Mr. Liu found himself charmed by the hidden balance of their bases, which belied their rounded bodies.

There were also plain vases with no images, perhaps only a running border near their throats, and while they were beautiful in their minimalist simplicity, he couldn't help but marvel at those with drawings. There were illustrations of flora and fauna, like birds, fishes, or horses; of supernatural entities like dragons or lions; of landscapes, like mountains, forests, streams, cloud-filled skies; of people, like farmers, fisherfolk, courtesans, artists.

But more than how they looked, Mr. Liu was held by their sounds. He trained himself to listen, and slowly the whispers turned into full voices. Each time he pulled a vase from its box, he heard and knew them for their individual inflections, and it became clear to him that each vase was known by its own song. He could now identify the music behind their initial murmurs, and it captivated him as nothing else ever had. In careful hurriedness, he lifted and changed the positions of the vases until he found an arrangement that provided the best harmony to his ear.

Awash in their music, he stood before his new purchases and drank in their songs.

* * *

'Sir,' Sally said one afternoon, the worry evident in the lines of her face. 'We don't have any more space. And frankly, everyone is afraid to move around in case we accidentally knock over and break a piece of your collection.'

Mr. Liu, with a wide Ming Dynasty soup bowl on his left, and a dipping dish—with a spoon—to his right, looked up from his desk with alarm.

'What? Break what?' he said.

Sally pressed. 'Sir, I'm afraid that it's a matter of "when" and not "if" that happens. There's also no more room for more items for your collection . . . unless you appropriate the warehouse too.'

'We're doing well, right?' he asked, lifting aside a small vase to find, then fiddle with, his computer keyboard to bring up the sales spreadsheets.

'Yes. We've been lucky. Orders are steady.' In fact, they were better than ever, and Sally attributed this to her boss's new calm. The retailers who ordered from him used to like Mr. Liu for his low prices and, well, nothing else. Now, they liked him for his low prices and his pleasant demeanour. Deep down she felt vindicated; she had always told others that all he needed was a hobby to transform him from a stern, rude, workaholic into a human being.

'Hmm . . . okay, good.'

'Sir?'

'I'll figure something out.'

Later that day, Mr. Liu told Sally to expect someone from the bank and to let him in for a private meeting. When the bank manager arrived—the same one who had given Mr. Liu his first vase; Sally found herself quite endeared with his leather satchel, his smile, his hello's—she hustled him quickly into Mr. Liu's room. He left two hours later, smiling even more broadly. The following day, Sally handed Mr. Liu a printed email detailing a loan for the purchase of the empty lot adjacent to their own. By the following week, Mr. Liu was meeting architects and building contractors. Once, before the door to Mr. Liu's room closed behind them, she noted the words 'Liu – six storey schematic' on the folder tucked under the arm of one of the architects.

Within eleven months, the six-storey schematic became an eight-storey building with two basement levels. With great effort, Mr. Liu, Sally, and everyone working in the company made it through the construction without their daily operations being hampered, but it took a lot of patience and compromise. The day the building opened was a big relief for all, and for Mr. Liu, most especially. Sally noticed the way her boss would surf the web for new vases, then visibly restrain himself from writing an email or picking up the phone by pulling his hands away and placing them to his side.

Sally wasn't asked to call for photographers, or to set up ribbons to be cut, or to prepare for a party on opening day; Mr. Liu had never been the type for fanfare. All that seemed to matter to him was that the time of restraint was finally over.

* * *

Fifteen years after he had heard his first vase, Mr. Liu added the 500th to his collection. It came cheap, but also with no papers, so its authenticity could not be proven without buying it; but the image the seller had emailed him had caught his eye. When he pulled it out of its packing, it was even more alluring than its photo.

The vase had a picture of a pale woman in traditional Chinese garb—flowing robes of white lined with yellow, blue, and green pastel trimmings, and wide sleeves that hid the woman's arms. She leaned on what was either an elaborately decorated staff, or a thin-bladed long sword sheathed in its ornamental scabbard. Her long, straight, ebony hair reached down to her hips. She was beautiful, but her beauty was not a soft or a kind one; there was strength held in check behind it. She stood on a trail of clouds, against the distant background of a wide earth and an expansive sky.

'Even more are needed.'

Mr. Liu, surprised, nearly dropped the vase. The words had flowed from the vase in a strong, female voice; not in song, but as a statement—it was the first time this had ever happened. He somehow brought himself to speak.

'More vases? Why?'

'The four pillars that hold up the heavens and protect the world cannot rely solely on the strength of turtle legs, no less the part of the pillar here. They are made stronger when fused with the voice and song of good people, whether they come of moulded clay or not.'

Mr. Liu did not understand. He tried to ask the vase more questions, but it did not reply and stayed mute, the lone silent piece in his collection.

* * *

Long years passed and were kind to Mr. Liu and his investments. Where his original office and warehouse once stood, there now rose a sixteen-storey edifice, one which dwarfed the eight-storey structure he had first built. His import business had grown with the turn of each year until he had become one of the top importers and wholesalers of cheaper electronics, machine parts, and appliances in the country. He had expanded into importing Asian décor, furniture, and yes, even antiquities, and he had been pleasantly surprised to find a steady, if small, local market for them.

He had married as well, after which he had moved to a quieter part of the city, not too far from his offices. Mr. Liu's wife had been a good woman who died too soon, but his son and daughter were devoted to him, and his five grandchildren were the image of their grandmother. He had lived a full life, a lucky life; there was little else an old man could ask for.

Mr. Liu knew he had purchased enough when he had bought vase number 1,356. That night, the woman on the vase came in his dreams. Goddess, Creator, Saviour, Mother, and Snake . . . he knew who she was by then, or at least suspected—it was not difficult to find references to the clues hidden in her words— but she did not acknowledge the name that escaped his lips. In fact, she did not speak at all, but pressed his forehead with a long-nailed finger, smiled, and faded away, leaving only the tingling sensation of her touch.

The vase collection was now stored on the twelfth floor of his new building. He had arranged them in ordered rows on specially made lacquered shelves, protected by glass, displayed in placements that he himself had directed. Sometimes, he would rearrange them, but not as often and not as radically as when he had been younger, having settled on a harmony he had grown accustomed to. His old age found him walking often between the shelves, ambling slowly down each aisle. To anyone else, the serene quiet was only disturbed by the soft shuffle of his footsteps and the tap-tap-tap of his cane.

* * *

The trip to Taipei was a gift from his son, Lawrence, who had gone on ahead and was already waiting for him there. When Lawrence had discovered that his father had never been to the National Palace Museum, he had taken it upon himself to bring Mr. Liu.

'Dad, you mean you've never seen their antiquities exhibit?' Both father and son, surprised at this, burst out laughing at the absurd discovery.

Mr. Liu's son was waiting for him as he exited baggage claim. 'It's early enough. Would you like to go to the museum now?' Lawrence asked. Mr. Liu nodded.

The taxi driver drove them up the main driveway, and Lawrence helped his father from the taxi. They walked through the wondrous archways that led to the stairs and up to the entrance for visitors and tourists.

The museum contained many ceramics, enough to make Mr. Liu giddy, as well as regretful that he had not visited the museum as a younger man. On display were not only vases, but bowls, pitchers, planters, cups, and washers, each with their own signature voices, each one as captivating as the next. He knew he could spend hours there, days even, and not tire of the sights or sounds.

Then he spied a vase displayed on a table near a section corner, away from the thickest part of the crowd, almost as to be ignored. It took him some time to recognize it; but when he did, his breath was taken away: its identical twin was the very first vase he had received from his bank so many years ago.

There was the garden that he had memorized over years of tireless scrutiny, there were the egrets and the lotus pond painted over the vase's white glaze, standing out starkly in shades of reds, yellows, greens, blues, and embellished gold. The waterweed, duckweed, and round leaves seemed to ripple in the azure pool they were painted upon. The tender green stems of the plants looked so real as to be swaying in a gentle breeze that blew close to the earth. Mr. Liu marvelled once more at the detail, the small butterflies that flitted about the light that struck the blooms in the artist's presentation of a lazy summer's morning, and the lotuses that stood forth all the more unsullied in contrast with the grey-brown soil from which they sprung.

It was an exact replica of his first vase, down to the minutest detail. Yet there was something strange about this one. Amid all the babble of the museum visitors, all the voices and songs of the other ceramics, this vase was silent. This vase did not sing. It was the first vase he had ever encountered without a voice; even the singular vase with the image of the Chinese lady had spoken to him that one time, many years ago. Mr. Liu stepped forward, marvelling still at its beauty, though extremely puzzled at the silence, a silence that spoke all the more loudly through a rising clamour that strangely included the thump of his excited heartbeat in his ears.

When Mr. Liu stood close enough, he reached out and touched the vase—and the garden scene startled him by coming to life before his eyes. The pool rippled as if the water was real, and the plants trembled delicately as if a slight breeze was blowing through them. The wings of the birds and the butterflies moved gracefully. He could feel the cool wind on his fingertips, and the hint of sunlight strengthened to an astounding, white brilliance that filled his view. The garden faded into this brightness, overwhelming his vision until the blinding whiteness was all he could see.

* * *

'Maybe it was the flight,' Lawrence said later. 'Maybe he was tired. I should have brought him to the hotel first.'

'Maybe it was his time.' his sister consoled him. 'Maybe you brought him to the museum just in time, before he left us.' Lawrence's lips accepted her consolation, but his mind relived his father's last moments once more.

He saw his father walking toward an exhibit that had caught his eye—everything normal, everything fine—reaching out slowly to an old vase. Lawrence had known that this might happen, and made to remind his father that touching was prohibited . . . when his father stiffened, then crumpled to the floor like a bursting sack of rice.

'Help! Help!' Lawrence had shouted, and rushed as fast as he could to his father's side, but by the time the museum staff arrived, he already knew that his father was gone.

Lawrence had not heard—no one could have, except for the man lying on the floor—but at that moment a new voice, that of one more good person, started to whisper, then sing, from the vase that just before had no song of its own, lending its support to that pillar of the world.

Cricket

Around *Tai mah*'s portrait rose tendrils of incense smoke, framing her visage in distinct waves of white curls. In their movement, they seemed more alive than the blank eyes and expression of the woman that the multiple red joss sticks had been lit for. They were much shorter now, having been burning for hours.

Unlike the smoke, the long lines of the family Chuang, extended family, and long-time friends and associates had long since dissipated. Everyone had made their obeisance, waved their sticks, and stuck them in the sand-filled pot. Everyone had caught up with each other, everyone's stories shared and told. The late, mid-afternoon lunch had been served—care of Lucy, from the heart of her domain, the kitchen—but dusk had fallen, and the leftover food had turned cold, which brought the last set of straggling visitors to their feet and to their goodbyes. It was a Saturday, and one year to the day, by the count on the lunar calendar, since the matriarch of the clan had passed into heaven, her age a venerable 108, the most long-lived of a long-lived set of sisters—even if the last eighteen had been spent in a senile cloud that never cleared. Come the end of dusk, the house at last turned quiet except for the clink of china and silverware from the back kitchen, the distant sounds of residual dishwashing by the house help.

Richard, Lucy, and their son, David, had retreated to the second floor of Tai mah's house; the hosts were tired, and Richard grumbled all the way upstairs about the burden of being the youngest son, whose role and misfortune had been to care for such a long-lived mother, and whose responsibilities stretched so even after death.

David, five and oblivious, played with a toy truck on the floor with his *yaya*. Lucy rested quietly on the couch, not even bothering to reach for the television remote control. She felt empty, and certainly did not have the energy to utter the words that would point out to her husband that she had played the role of host for the guests more, while he concentrated on his friends, brothers, and bottles of whiskey; that she had cooked and baked in the hot kitchen since early that morning while he slept; that while his brothers and sisters had indeed moved out years before when they were all much younger, and he, the *sho-ti*, had been the one obliged to stay behind, he had been the one to inherit his mother's house—quite a large one. Now that she was gone, it was all theirs, even if it had taken 108 years for it to happen. They could sell it and move to a smaller, more manageable space, one they would own, she wanted to say, to leave behind all his complaints, and the weight of all her memories. But despite his misery, Richard never talked about moving, and so she left the words on her tongue, which became heavier with the time that passed and time that was still to come.

By nine-thirty that evening, everyone in the household lay in bed, even the home help; they had only bothered to watch one episode of a soap opera on the small TV provided for them in the back kitchen before turning in; they were that exhausted. The living room, which led to the dining area with a large lauriat table—beyond which were the sliding doors that, when open, extended to the veranda and a garden—lay quiet. This was where all the guests had mingled, laughed, and talked; but now, the air hung still, as the joss sticks burned down, small, ember-red eyes glowing in the dark. Slowly, each one burned to a stub. When the last one winked out, dropping its ash-tip onto the pot's sand, when the last of the curls of incense smoke wafted up and vanished before the eyes on Tai mah's portrait, a black cricket chirped and made its way forward from behind the pot.

From what little filtered in from the outside, its carapace caught light and reflected back a soft sheen. Moving forward, antennae trembling, it chirped once more, leaped forward, and landed on a high shelf with a photograph of Tai mah when she was much younger, and then, after dropping its head in a bow, sighed, sounding very much like a person who was resigned to some daunting task.

* * *

Richard's voice half-caught in his throat, which gave him a chance to change what he was about to say. Masking the many words he had intended with a cough, he instead only said, 'Yes,' and hastily took his cup and gulped several mouthfuls of coffee.

'Furthermore,' said the cricket, in front of a seemingly stoic Lucy and a laughing, amused David, 'you would do well to stop all your drinking, you and your brothers. I'm glad that none of you ever got into smoking. The smell! Heaven should be grateful for small blessings, few as they are.'

The cricket had made its appearance at breakfast in the kitchen, dropping from somewhere above and startling the family. It had chirped its greeting: 'Good morning.' Lucy was the first to recover and greet it back—then, in a split second, blush at the absurdity of it all—but her embarrassment was immediately replaced with acceptance. David just smiled and clapped his hands. Richard took the longest to come to himself, before unfurling the newspaper he had crumpled in his hands. The cricket sniffed and addressed Richard immediately about his eating habits; before him was a plate of fried, fatty sausages and a double-heaping of rice, presenting itself like the evidence of a crime.

'This was prepared by Lucy!' Richard had replied, shifting the blame.

'Yes, every day,' remarked the cricket, 'on your instructions.' A darkness touched Richard's heart at that moment, a fear he thought he had escaped, or at the very least, could ignore.

'And you,' the cricket said to Lucy, no less firm, but with just a hint of kindness, 'you may want to use that head of yours a bit more!' Lucy was taken aback, having expected some other kind of rebuke. In her mind lay the notion that she was the ideal wife, one who had been there for years even before her wedding. But for some reason, whether it was the timing of the cricket's words—that she was, for that morning, for that very moment, in the appropriate frame of mind and heart—or whether it was the way the cricket said it, she began to question where exactly she stood in the frame of her marriage. Instead of finding herself feeling any number of emotions that she otherwise could have expected, she instead found herself, strangely enough, uplifted with hope. Granted, it was only a small hope, less than a spark, but she liked it enough to consider ways to feed it.

The cricket turned to David.

'You are a happy one,' it said. David, as if in agreement, laughed louder. 'But isn't everyone, at your age?'

The cricket surprised them all when it took a long hop and landed on David's bare arm. It brushed its antennae gently on the young boy's skin. Up close and given the insect's size—it easily covered half of David's forearm—it was quite fearsome-looking. Its mandibles were sharp, and its legs, thorny stems that ended in clawed hooks. It was all angles, points, and sharp edges, and gave the impression that it was in a constant state of bristling. But where Lucy held her breath at how close it was to her son, and where Richard's hands tightened into fists and his body tensed in apprehension, David showed no fear, no sense of any danger. He just smiled at the cricket, and even dared to reach out and reciprocate by stroking with his fingers the length of its body. Lost in his touch was the natural roughness of a young child, replaced by what could have been affection.

'Hello,' David said to it.

'Well!' the cricket replied. 'Let's see how you all are, then.' It hopped back onto the table, then off, and disappeared into the kitchen's darker recesses and crevices. For the rest of the morning, it popped up with its comments and complaints, to further surprise the family as they went about their business.

* * *

Lucy nearly dropped the lid of the wok she was cooking in when the cricket hopped from the floor to the table beside her hot stove. It remarked right away that it found her too sullen. 'You are doing something you do well,' it said. 'And yet, you do not smile. Why do it, then?' It hopped away to perch on a ledge near the ceiling, overlooking the entire kitchen.

This time, Lucy found within herself a sense of rising to the challenge of the cricket's question. She began moving with more vigour around the kitchen, actually banging her ladles and utensils against the wok, chopping food for lunch with force, stirring and frying with an energy she did not usually exert, cooking with insistence. What she was insisting on she did not know, but she acted in defence of herself, of who she was, and while doing so, she began, as the cricket commented, using her head.

She was not unintelligent; she had been near the top of her class when she was a student, though she did only a couple of years' work as a teller at a local bank before she married Richard. They had met through their parents' mutual friend, and knew each other for nearly a year before the marriage had been settled, agreed upon by both of them and their parents. It seemed so natural. She was no great beauty, and her family was not rich, so she knew her prospects were narrow. Richard seemed like a nice enough man, six years her senior, though she did not like the way he scratched himself in places when he thought no one was looking, or the way she caught him slipping off his shoes under the dinner table to curl his toes. He said the right things, to her parents as well as to her. The issue of him being the youngest in a family of six boys and five girls came up only once, but her parents, particularly her mother, brushed it aside as unimportant. She had not known what to think of marrying a youngest son, and so thought nothing of it herself, until the days after her wedding stretched into the weeks, months, and years of being anchored to a filial duty that her husband resented and infected her with. Looking back now, it had not been so bad after all; she learned to cook from her mother-in-law, and became as good, if not better, than her. When the older woman became too old to cook, the kitchen became hers.

For the first time in a long time, she smelled the spices from the steaming food in front of her, tasted their sharp tangs, and broke into a smile that took years of lines and inherited bitterness from her face.

* * *

David sat on the living room floor alternately reading his picture books and playing with scattered toys. When his *yaya* saw that he was behaving, she left him to help outside in the garden with hooking the laundry onto the clotheslines, still within sight of him but separated by some distance and the sliding glass-panelled doors. The cricket made itself visible across the floor from him; he smiled at it but did not move towards it. Instead, David picked up a book and read aloud from it, as if to no one in particular but really intending for the cricket to hear his words. The insect inched closer and closer, and when it was near, David allowed it to perch itself on top of his shoulder. He finished the book, and another. By the end of the fifth book, the cricket found itself on the coffee table, on a level with David's eyes. They regarded each other quietly. They did not need to exchange any words. The cricket watched David, aware of his youth, and to its eyes he seemed like a clean blank sheet of paper on which anything could be drawn or written.

* * *

Since breakfast, Richard had moved restlessly around the house. He could not stay still, moving from the ground floor to the second and back down again, consciously wandering between rooms and sections of the house that were empty. He avoided the kitchen, knowing his wife was there; he did the same for outdoors, where the home help was busy; he passed by his son, who was sitting on the living room floor engrossed in his books and toys, several times, and paid him no mind.

The feeling of dread had magnified since the cricket's first appearance. He could not lay a finger on or say clearly what he feared, but he sensed some impending trepidation, a moment of reckoning that he had to face, and he knew he was not ready and would most certainly be found wanting. As to why, he could not say. But he blamed the cricket.

Eventually, he chose his sanctuary in the small, corner stockroom he had converted into a home-office many years ago. He would normally never enter this room on a Sunday, but today he found himself walking into it. He shut the door behind him and sat at his desk, settling into an old, fraying, office chair. The desk was covered in old receipts and invoices, correspondence, and office bric-a-brac that had piled up over time. Many of the documents were on matters that were long overdue for his attention, which he continued to procrastinate on and did not even glance at. Instead, he sat back, put his hands behind his head, closed his eyes, and resolved to forget the morning and the cricket through an activity he often engaged himself in: self-pity.

He thought about money, how little he had and how dependent he was on the salary he was given from the family business, run by his *Ahiya*—eldest brother—and his wife, who controlled its finances. How all his other brothers seemed to be doing better, whether in their own professions or their private, family lives. How they all seemed to be able to travel and go to different places as they pleased, while he had to wait to be invited so that he could share rooms and meals and other accommodations to fit his shoestring budget. How his sisters seemed to have married into what they wanted, for the most part, but really, their lives did not matter so much to him as his brothers', in comparison. He laughed and put up a front when he was before them, of course—nothing was wrong, everything was all right, I'm doing fine, I can handle this, I'm content. All his worries he would never admit to anyone, but he blamed the secret unfairness of it all on his being the youngest in the family, neither for the first time, nor the last. Why must the burden of being left behind to care for the ageing parents always fall on him? He let the self-pity wash over him, mixing it with the images of his brothers in their own homes, his sisters with their husbands, and the pity and scorn he believed he saw in their eyes, and yes, even in their children's eyes, whenever they saw him. There was no respect there, he was certain of it, even when they greeted him with smiles and hugs.

What had his *Achi*, his eldest sister, once said about him? That he was the slowest and most dim-witted of them all. The duty of tutoring all of them through school fell to his eldest sister, and he recalled how strict she was with all of them. She expected nothing but good grades, saying how important it was for their future, but it was with a forlorn expression that he would often watch his other siblings leave the study table ahead of him, yes, even his youngest sister, the flighty, bubble-headed one who had gone against her father, shunned the Chinese-Filipino he had asked her to meet, and instead married a Swiss-Canadian; even she seemed to be better off in Canada, a first-world country.

It was so unfair that many of his siblings needed so little effort to pass their exams while he would spend hours, hungry and past dinner, studying and memorizing, only to do poorly on his tests.

Achi shouted and scolded and put up her hands in exasperation, and come high school he finally shouted back. She left him then to his own devices, and it took him five years to pass high school instead of four, and a bit longer to get through college. But he got through! Yet, it seemed as nothing compared to how well everyone else had done. Achi. She was a successful accountant, and the way she remained distant from him ever since he broke off from her stood out in stark contrast to the way she comported herself with the others.

'Perhaps,' the cricket chirped from an upper shelf where boxes of old car parts had been stored, 'you would be better off humbling yourself instead of presenting yourself so highly.'

Richard opened his eyes, found the insect, and glared at it. 'What would you know?'

'Enough. Much. Too much,' the cricket said. 'Even you must admit that for all your posturing, your siblings know the truth.'

'How could you know?' Richard said. He felt his blood rising to his face.

The cricket ignored the question. 'Many of your brothers are the same as you. They are not the same as their outward appearances of success. Behind their public faces, they have great failings in their homes. You may draw consolation from this, but in truth, it is a tragedy, because you, your family, are all the same.

'Why not humble yourself?' the cricket repeated. 'For your sake. For your wife's. For your son. Never mind your siblings, for now, but you would be much happier for it.'

'You leave my son out of this!'

'He is a good boy. He could be successful, in the right way. Don't infect him with your bitterness!'

Richard could no longer control himself. He felt his rage rise at the insolence of the insect who dared to speak to him in this manner. He reached for the nearest object—a mug used as a pen holder—stood up in a rush, which sent his chair crashing against the wall, and threw the mug at the cricket with all his might.

His aim was off, and the mug crashed and broke into many pieces just to the right of its target. An explosion of pens and white ceramic burst and fell to the floor. The cricket jumped and fled, squeezing through a small hole in the upper corner of the doorway and out into the main portion of the house.

Richard flung the door open and gave chase, brandishing one of his slippers. He limped quickly after the cricket, one foot unshod, swinging his arm at the cricket in wild, violent arcs and screaming invectives at it. The cricket flew fast to the left, to the right, avoiding Richard, leaping and flying as fast as it could for dear life. Richard, throwing all caution away, went after it, hitting and bumping his body against furniture and shelves, toppling them over and sending picture frames, vases, books, and appliances crashing to the marble floor.

The noise brought Lucy from the kitchen, her mouth agape in shock and fear. She ran for her husband to try and hold him back, but when she saw him follow the cricket into the living room, taking a swing that dealt a glancing blow to David's forehead, she forgot everything else and gathered her wailing son into her arms and carried him to the corner of the room, shielding him with her body.

All the doors and windows were closed; there was nowhere for the cricket to run. It flew as high as it could, from one upper corner to another, but Richard's rage fuelled him and gave him strength beyond what energy the insect could maintain in escape. It flew much more slowly, and much lower, leapt in slower flight, until, with a mighty swing, Richard connected at last with a satisfying thwack, sending the cricket smashing against the wall. It fell to the ground, and Richard was upon it, bringing his slipper down on it again and again, shouting incoherently all throughout until he could no longer lift his arms and needed to stop, to at last draw in great deep breaths for his tired body. The cricket lay at his feet, a mess of yellowish-green viscous fluid mixed with the smashed mess of its crushed body.

'What did you do?' Lucy screamed, cradling David's head against her chest. 'Why did you kill it?' The bump on David's forehead was turning into an angry red. He struggled hysterically against his mother, reaching out with his hands and arms for the cricket; it was all she could do to hold him.

'Shut up!' Richard shouted back. 'Just shut up! And shut him up, too!'

'Why did you kill it?' she repeated. 'David liked the cricket! We could have kept it for him!'

Richard did not immediately answer. Instead, he turned away. The anger, spent like a volcanic eruption, was leaving him. He felt drained of energy, but not of the dread and fear. No, those remained, like a loaded gun still aimed and readied against his chest. He could not explain what he did, or why. But his pride and bitterness—and yes, his self-pity—those he did not even try to push away.

'He'll get over it,' Richard said to Lucy, and he put all the cold arrogance he could muster into his words.

Something hit him on his head. It hurt, but only slightly, not enough to cause him to even shout out. He turned and saw his son standing defiantly up against him, one foot also unshod, his face a mask of hatred and anger. The slipper he had thrown at his father lay on the floor and to the side after having bounced off Richard's head.

Richard stared at the thrown slipper, then at his son, and then he could only stumble in a daze back to his home-office. The dread and fear inside him increased with each step, and even when he closed the door behind him, he knew that it would not be enough to keep his tragedy away.

The Singing Contest

The plaza was boisterous, colourful, and happy, as well it should have been: Today was the town's feast day, and the fiesta was in full swing.

Quick-tempo music blared from giant, black speakers atop tall platforms positioned at the plaza's four corners. Banners and miniature flags—shaped from every available scrap of paper, plastic, and cloth, and dyed in this year's official colours of red and yellow—hung from a spider-web of criss-crossing string and rope, hovering over the plaza in a net-like weave that, though unplanned, was not unattractive, and which contrasted sharply with the green of the trees, the blue of the sky. Only the piece of the heavens directly above the sprawling wooden stage erected to the front of the plaza was spared from being covered so. People had begun to fill the empty space from as early as two in the afternoon. The food and drink drew them, as did the music, but everyone anticipated the entertainment and the contests the most.

The poorer folk—the maids and the other home help, the fishermen from the next town near the sea, the drivers of the jeepneys and tricycles, the farmers, and all their families—took up more than half the plaza but to the rear, the vicinity furthest from the stage. Where they weren't, the area had been cordoned off by waist-high posts lashed together with steel wire; but to keep even this separation festive, someone had attractively adorned the wires with banners, too. In this special area at the front, seats had been set out for the important folk: the richest, the respected, the learned, the prominent, the elected, and their guests from out-of-town; but the poorer folk were not unhappy with this arrangement. This was the way it was, and they were more than content to mingle and laugh and talk and joke with each other in unbridled merriment, to forget the drudgery of the ordinary days, and to partake of all that had been prepared: beer for the men and some women, sodas and juices for the children, and a plethora of viands, staples, and desserts. They were laid for everyone—tens of tens of *litsong baka at baboy, adobong manok at pusit,* orange-hued *palabok* in giant *bilaos,* steaming *sinangag* by the kettles, homemade cakes and sweets, and barbecues grilled from all manners of meat.

Invading the scene in one corner were the stalls of two fast-food chains, one that sold hamburgers, the other, pizzas, but in the true fashion of the people they were welcomed and not ignored, and the younger ones seemed to enjoy their presence. All the delicious aromas mixed and wafted in the air with the sounds of celebration, but there was more than that—the air was filled with contentment and plenty. Today was the town's feast day; the year 1994 had been good, and low spirits had no place here.

The contests! The highlight of any self-respecting town fiesta—along with the parade, of course, but that was over and done with, the procession of saints and Marias dressed in all their finery having moved behind the scenes—the contests created a buzz among the revellers. The beauty pageant, nearly finished, had just paraded their finalists out onto the stage in their full regalia, even if the combination of late afternoon humidity and bright stage lights made the atmosphere much too hot.

Seated near the front of the stage and more than a few rows beyond the wired posts, with a visiting *balikbayan* family whose patriarch originally hailed from the town on one side, and the town's oldest and most distinguished attorney and his family on the other, sat the Master, his wife, and his friends. His watchful bodyguards sat on a nearby bench, just a short distance away.

'Resplendent! Gorgeous! Enchanting! Enamouring!' said the most distinguished attorney in a loud voice. A man of the law, he was also a man with a large vocabulary, and did his best to exhibit his way with words whenever he could. His wife heard him, and as he intended, so did many of those around him, including the Master, but she did not take her eyes off the stage; she just sighed without exhibiting that she was doing so, a skill she had mastered over her years of wedded bliss.

The Master and his friends laughed. The beauty contestants this year were indeed everything the attorney had described. Beauties, all. But the Master, like many of the townsfolk, had his mind on the next event, the amateur singing contest; on a particular contestant, in fact, and said so with a conviction and excitement he usually reserved for his more ferocious fighting cocks.

'This year, my friends, God has been good to our town,' he said, falling into the semi-speech that those who are used to being attended to have a tendency to do. 'Our tobacco harvests are thick and plentiful, there have been no great floods, and everyone is happy and has money. Why, even my gardener's son, who gathers the grass after his father cuts them, has bought new shoes this year. Not slippers, shoes! But I count not the least among our blessings—among *my* blessings—to have in my household the most wonderful singer I have ever heard in my life!'

This was not the first time the Master had waxed eloquent about this singer whom he safeguarded. Those among his closer friends who had been invited to his house for private parties knew of her. These friends nodded their heads in full agreement, while others not so close inched nearer in the hopes of shortening their distance from the Master, their ears perked and their eyes alight with interest. The Master's wife, bored with the pageant, raised her head and sat tall in her seat to rush her opinion forward.

'Mariafe is more than wonderful. She is an angel! And just sixteen years old! To think it was an accident when we first heard her. When was this, Andres? Some years ago? All I remember was that it was your birthday.' She knew how to prompt him after so many years of wedded bliss.

'It was my birthday,' the Master said, glancing at his wife briefly then turning to the stage with a blank but dramatic, faraway gaze as if lost in memory. On the stage, the master of ceremonies, a showbiz celebrity hired from Manila for the occasion, announced the finalists of the beauty pageant while bidding the losers goodbye and thank you, but not without sending them off with the consolation of a parting buss on the cheek, or a light caress to the hips as his blessing for their having joined.

'Yes, it was,' the Master said again, 'and she sang for me the sweetest Happy Birthday song. She has been singing for me every birthday since, and even when it isn't my birthday I ask her to sing for me. I am glad to have thought of entering her in the singing contest this year!'

Her prompting done, the Master's wife had a sudden change of mood and sat back into her chair with a discernible huff. She did not contradict her husband—another one of her marriage skills—and say that the idea was not his but *hers*, and did not mutter under her breath that Mariafe would have joined the contest years earlier if not for the fact that the Master had been selfishly keeping the young waif and her talent for himself alone. The idea to enter her in the town fiesta's singing contest took four years to germinate in the infertile soil of his stubborn brain, and he had put it off with many a wave of the hand, many a turned back and a grunt, and many an exasperated exclamation of 'Perhaps, next year!', until she had slyly suggested that letting people know that he was Mariafe's benefactor would add prestige to the family name, an additional generosity that he could lay a claim of fame to.

'How did you discover her, sir?' said a modern and brave young man seated nearby. He was the son of a man who did business with the Master, and he knew his father wished for some deeper business intimacy with him. This young man's father, seated beside his son, nodded his head in enthusiastic agreement to the question.

'Truly, it was an accident,' the Master said. 'We had taken her in, an orphan, a relative of a relative of one of our home help. To think she had been living in my house all this time, under my nose.' His wife whipped out her fan and decided to turn her attention back to the pageant, where the contestants had been whittled down to the last four. Amid all the noise, the blare of the speakers, the shouts, the other ongoing conversations, and the host's insistent voice, it was only the Mistress among those revolving around the Master who feigned disinterest. And why not? She knew the story he was about to tell quite well, but the *balikbayans* and the attorney's family did not, so they listened to him with rapt attention. Perhaps the Master didn't notice the growing attention, or perhaps he did; his eyes, nonetheless, retained their faraway look, lost in distant reminiscing.

'That day was one of the worst birthdays of my life,' the Master said. 'We had decided on a small party then, just my family and a few close friends. A few of you were there, were you not? That year, if you remember, was a bad one. Too hot. Not enough rain. The tobacco grew pale and thin. And my birthday meal was horrendous! I was upset with the cook. There were not enough vegetables, and what she served was tasteless and stringy. And the chicken was so undercooked I could not chew through it. Very tough, it was. Thankfully, for dessert, I had ordered a cake from the bakeshop, so that saved us, but the meal itself . . . ay!'

Those around clucked their tongues in pity.

'The cook blamed someone, of course, and that someone was my Mariafe, my angel! But she was not yet my angel at that time. The cook claimed that she had sent Mariafe out before dawn to buy food at the market, but that the little girl returned at eleven.'

'It's so hard to find good help,' said the young man's father.

'Children will be children,' the Master said defensively, with a tone of finality. The young man's father resolved that it would be better for him to keep his thoughts to himself from then on, but to his credit, managed to keep his smile and his nodding head.

'The cook should've bought it herself the day before,' the Mistress said, saving the young man's father somewhat.

'Yes, yes, well, she has been with us since *lolo's* time, dearest,' the Master replied more gently, meeting his match.

'You should retire her,' the Mistress said.

'In any case,' the Master continued, ignoring his wife so as to steer the conversation back to himself, 'Mariafe had been gone for too long, leaving too little time for the cook to prepare lunch properly. What's more, she returned with too little of what the cook had ordered, and had spent too much. She wasted my money!' The Master said this with thunder in his voice. His friends chuckled in polite mirth, knowing the Master well enough to recognize his mock anger. They knew that losing money in this way did not bother the Master at all, though it might have very well upset them if such a thing had happened in their households.

'Oh, the cook was partly to blame. Why did she send a young girl for this job? Why did she wait till the final minute to buy the food? But I couldn't say much to her. She has been with us since forever, and she has gotten old. I pitied her, and Mariafe. But the young girl needed to know punishment, and was sent to wash the dishes by herself. No one was to help her. An apt consequence, with more to follow, surely.

'And so the day would have mercifully ended, if I had not suddenly heard a wonderful sound. As soon as I blew the candles on my cake, just as everyone finished singing Happy Birthday, the song continued, faintly, like a lost echo, and I looked but no one around me was singing any more. I wondered if I was going crazy, if I was the only one who could hear the song, but the looks on everyone else's faces told me that they could hear it too. I stood up and tracked the song to the far end of the kitchen. To the very back, mind you, and that is not a short walk! I discovered her! *I*. It was Mariafe, singing the Happy Birthday song! But it sounded different, nothing like what we are used to hearing, something like . . . just . . . oh . . . something more delightful . . . a different version, sweet, touching . . . ah! It is hard to describe. I am running out of words.'

'Elegant? Entrancing? Exquisite?' the distinguished attorney volunteered.

'Yes, yes. Never mind. You will hear it for yourselves later when she gets on stage,' the Master said with some testiness. He had grown accustomed to the attention, and was aware of the slight shift, so he said in a louder voice: 'She was singing for *me*! How wonderful! Here was this little girl, elbow-deep in dirty dishwater singing Happy Birthday for me! My heart melted, and I took her away from the dirty plates and made her sing for me again in front of everyone.'

'She was terrified,' the Master's wife said dryly.

'At first! At first!' the Master said. 'But when I made her sing again she forgot all her fear, and her voice made me forget my horrible lunch. Since then, I have enjoyed her singing as often as I can. She knows many songs, some even I don't know. I asked her once where she had learned them. She just smiled back and said she picked them up here and there, but I really don't need to know! I just want to listen. Her voice, there is magic in it. And now, I have entered her into the contest, paid for her dress and her fee with my own money, my angel, my Mariafe, so that I can share her talent with everyone! When will she sing, dearest?'

'She is the first,' the Mistress answered, though she knew that the Master already knew that, since it was he who had requested this from the contest organizers. He was not the Master for nothing, and he always got what he wanted. 'Why bother with the other inferior talents?' the Master had exclaimed to her weeks before. He was so confident of Mariafe, he did not bother to seek out the contest's judges, wherever they were seated, not even their names.

'Good! The sooner we hear her the better, and we need not waste our time with the others,' he said, echoing his older sentiment. 'They will be nothing in comparison, and will probably not even bother taking the microphone after hearing my angel!' The Master sighed. 'When will this pageant end?'

'It just did, sir,' said the young man. 'Look, they are crowning the winner. She is lovely!'

'Not half as lovely as the voice of my angel,' the Master said. Without looking down, and without losing his toothy grin, the young man's father turned his right foot outward so as to step on his son's left, as if to say, *that is enough*. In such a packed space, so tight and crowded, nobody saw him do this, not even the young man, though he surely felt it.

* * *

In the main crowd, behind the wired posts, but as close to the stage as she could approach, the cook waited, anxious for Mariafe and her first performance in public.

She had been bragging to everyone she knew—and to more than a few that she did not—about the young girl. Her proclamation: 'Mariafe is my protege, my ward, my apprentice!' Why, when she herself was young she used to carry a fair tune; but when life became heavy and she could not find the time to cultivate her singing, she had taught Mariafe instead, whom she had protected from the hardships of life so that her talent could be nurtured. This story the cook told had found its way to truth in her mind; in fact, Mariafe was just the daughter of a second-cousin's cousin who had died early in life and the two had never met till Mariafe was sent to work for the Master when the girl had turned eleven.

'I love her like a daughter,' the Cook had told everyone, 'and I will not see her gift wasted by the needs of life, like mine was.' Someone asked if she herself could still sing, and the cook gave in to the mild insistence and screeched out a *kundiman* in her youth, which left the listeners seeking some certainty, asking the cook if, indeed, Mariafe was or was not her direct blood-relative, with the reluctantly given latter answer providing them the assurance they sought.

The cook had used that afternoon to spread her story further, so that by the time the pageant ended, a buzz of anticipation spread through the main crowd. Who was this little girl, Mariafe, dear to the Master's old cook and sheltered so protectively in his house?

Yet, now that Mariafe's debut was imminent, the cook felt some apprehension. In her heart she felt shame that she did not share the Master's confidence in the girl's gifts. Expectations ran high—she had some fault in that, though she would never admit it—and experience had taught her that in such times a fall is ripe. Singing at home, for the Master, his family, and his guests was so different from singing in front of so many strangers. The stage looked incomprehensibly large to the old cook's eyes. What would Mariafe do, faced with a crowd like this? She felt her knees buckle, not as much for the girl as for her own reputation, now latched to the upcoming performance.

On the Master's birthday those many years ago, when everyone had heard Mariafe sing in that lovely voice for the very first time, the cook remembered suddenly that it was also the girl's birthday, on the same day as the Master's. It struck her then that the girl must have been singing for herself, in self-pity, having to wash the dishes all by herself in punishment. But the cook had never told the Master this, allowing him the fantasy that what he had heard was a song dedicated to him. Since then, the cook had moved Mariafe's birthday to a month later, to protect the Master, his heart having been touched so, and unwittingly protecting Mariafe as well.

'Where's your Mariafe?' someone in the crowd, an old friend of the cook's, called out to her.

'Be patient!' the cook responded tersely, sensitive, taking the question as a personal slight and craning her neck for a better view of the stage.

'When will this contest start?' someone else asked. The cook was aware of the crowd, the heat, the restlessness, and the noise. *Will Fe even be heard over this din?* she thought.

'I ate five pieces of chicken!'

'I do not think this year's winner is as pretty as last year's or even the year before.'

'*I* like her. I like her *very* much.'

The noise and different conversations increased, and the people remained inattentive when the cook saw Mariafe walk out in a pink dress of many frills and laces, which the cook herself had chosen from the *palengke*. From where the cook stood, Mariafe looked so small, and the stage so wide and deep. The host introduced her, a long winded-speech focusing on the girl's youth.

'Where's my wallet?' a man to the right of the cook exclaimed. 'I think someone took my wallet!' A commotion grew as people looked into each other's faces for a culprit.

'How old are you?' the host asked after announcing Mariafe's name over the microphone.

'Sixteen, *kuya*,' Mariafe said.

'This year's Queen *is* prettier than last year's!'

'No, she's not!'

'Is this your first time participating in a singing contest?'

'Why did you eat so much chicken? You look sick!'

'Yes, *kuya*.'

'Is that Mariafe? She's so small!'

'Where's my wallet? Where's my wallet?'

'How does it feel to be competing against more experienced singers?'

'Shh! Never mind about your wallet!'

'The song doesn't know how old I am, *kuya*.'

'Why are you defending her so? Is this year's pageant winner your girlfriend?'

'That's true! That's true! Words of wisdom from such a young lady!'

The cook sweated profusely where she stood, from heat and nervousness. The host introduced Mariafe's song, a popular ditty from years back. The song was a love ballad, the kind that the simple people of the town had a taste for, of little sophistication and perhaps too much sentimentality, but which spoke of the raw, simple attraction and romance that they, and everyone, simple or not, had experienced at one time or another in their lives, a song that even the jaded can remember with a wry smile. The host mentioned Mariafe's name again and stepped back to leave the stage to the singer. Over the speakers, the song's opening bars began from some hidden music player.

'You! You were jostling me a while ago! You took my wallet!'

'In fact, yes, she *is* my girlfriend!'

'You're right. I feel sick. Maybe the chicken was spoiled.'

'I didn't take your wallet!'

'Liar!'

The cook saw the small figure of Mariafe raise the microphone to her face. She opened her mouth, and the first notes came forth from her throat, wafting through the air, beginning a dream.

They listened, the cook, the Master, the Mistress, and all those around them—the man who ate too much chicken and the man without a wallet; the thief, who paused in his surreptitious getaway some few feet away; the ones debating the worthiness of this year's pageant winner, and the winner herself, backstage; the other contestants, from the beauty pageant and from the singing contest; the host, and the food-sellers. They all did more than listen. They heard.

At the end of the dream, they awoke. The cook realized with surprise that her face was wet. So did the Master's wife, and a number of other men and women. The Master found something stuck in his throat but gurgled it away before someone caught him. He wanted to say, 'Didn't I tell you so? Didn't I say she was an angel? This was better than anything else I've ever heard! This was better than she's ever sung!' but in spite of himself he found a miniscule measure of prudence somewhere inside and uttered not a word. Or perhaps that small bit of prudence squeezed away any words he could have said before he could speak them. The same could be said of the distinguished attorney, who forgot his extensive vocabulary for that moment; when later that night he tried to describe to himself what he had heard, he found that he could not, and his wife was spared from producing any more sighs.

The applause came, disguised at first in the dress of an initial, light sprinkling, as uncertain as a shower in summer, before bursting into sudden thunder, lightning, and rain—long, loud, and lasting, a veritable downpour, a forceful series of mighty sheets and waves. Mariafe bowed and made way for the next singer, disappearing backstage where the deluge would not wash over her. She walked past the host who, in slack-jawed incredulity, wondered desperately where he could find a telephone so he could call his agent in Manila. He needed to tell someone, anyone, about what he had just heard, but could only fumble clumsily with his microphone.

Clapping was all anybody could do for a while, until hands raw and red could not be brought together any more. The second contestant, a young man in his mid-twenties, took the stage timidly, but the audience would not even let him speak, let alone sing; they hooted and cheered, and they called Mariafe out for another song. 'One more! One more!' they chanted. The host took his microphone and asked for them to calm down, invoking the turns of the other contestants, but he could not be heard over the din. He himself fought only half-heartedly for the other singers as Mariafe's voice still lingered in his ears; he did not want any other voice to come and take its place.

The Master had been correct—the contest ended right then and there. Mariafe did not return, but the audience refused to let her go. They stayed, they shouted, they screamed, but suddenly afraid, she did not come out. Rushing to the stage in their adoring frenzy, the crowd moved forward, daring to cross the breach that separated them from the privileged; the wired posts tipped over, and the divide gave way. Through the shock and the frightened screams borne of this unexpected violation, the Master kept his head and ordered his bodyguards to rescue Mariafe, to bring her home, but it was all they could do to fight the crush mobbing the narrow staircase that led backstage.

In the end, the Master's men succeeded even over the rabble with their strength and ferocity, plucking the girl from those who wished to have all of her for themselves. They shielded her with their thick bodies and ran, lifting her into the Master's waiting vehicle, and speeding her away with a screech of tyres. They succeeded, but not without being hurt themselves, as was evident by their torn clothing, their multitudinous bruises and bleeding cuts. Later, one of them would need attention from a doctor for an infected cut over his eye, and another would limp for a week from a sprained ankle.

But even after Mariafe's rescue, the stage, front and back, remained overrun. She was never declared the winner; in the chaos, the wires to the sound and electrical systems had been ripped from their sockets, and all the speakers and lights had died. The host, in true melodrama as would befit himself, his business, and perhaps all the people running wildly around him, held his arms out in the middle of the stage and declared as loud as he could, 'A star is born!'

During the initial rush, the Master, his wife, and his friends had fortunately retreated to the safety of a temporary space to the left of the stage. They stood behind a makeshift barrier of plywood that served as a divide for the stage props. If they noticed that they shared the same area with the instruments and costumes for the town's marching band, improvised racks upon which hung a myriad gowns and jackets, and gaudy papier-mâché props of all shapes, colours, and sizes, they gave no sign. This space had become their sanctuary, having been spared the attention of the mob. Somehow, the cook had also found her way there with them. She sat on a wooden crate, fanning herself with a piece of cardboard she had picked up off the ground while massaging her right leg, which had been hurt when she had tripped and fallen. Though the danger of the crush had passed, they were still breathless and edgy. They could not even talk; all they could do was wait.

The fiesta ended like the *sawa* firecrackers set off during the afternoon parade, in a huge explosion of violence and noise. The mob was the smoke cloud left behind; after the explosion, it thinned first around the edges, faded to the middle, and as the plaza emptied, dissipated when each person found himself, then went his own way. The wind picked up, setting the banners above to rustle and wave, but in the gloom they had lost all colour. Chairs and benches lay overturned, and spilled food and drinks, wrappers, and plastic bags littered the scene. There were many articles of clothing on the ground: a torn shirt here, a hat there, and countless solo shoes and slippers scattered across the scene, missing their partners.

The plaza turned quiet but was still unsettled. Mariafe's voice still lingered in the minds of all who had heard her. They knew something had happened to each of them after hearing her song, yet no one could erase the feeling that they had not been prepared for it, and that somehow, they had all been found undeserving.

When You Let It Go

The Limp and his gang are after us, and we don't even know what we have done. There are four of us: Scaler, Kicks, Tri, and me. There are five of them, and they're all beasts. None of them are small. None of us are big.

No mistaking it, the threat is real. Earlier this morning, the Limp and his second caught Scaler's eye while the teacher's back was turned. He raised his fist, grimaced or smiled—we never could tell when he is doing which—and then his second pointed down at the table with a fat, grimy finger.

'What'd we do? What'd we do?' Tri squealed in fear during recess. We escaped them briefly as soon as the bell rang by joining the crowd as fast as we could. The Limp is dumb, but not too dumb to know that we like hanging out in the library, so now we're where we think he would never imagine us going: the playground. Everybody else is in their spots, so we find ourselves awkwardly standing by a dirty wall, beside a can of garbage, knowing fully well that this is not our place. A basketball hits my back and someone I don't know comes to get it but not before giving me a sneer. The playground is noisy, dusty, humid, and safe, but only for the moment. The Limp's sure to find out where we are.

'Somebody's been telling stuff about us,' Kicks says with a voice so soft and gentle. His father's a top official in the local government, so he has the least to fear. We know Kicks' father and the Limp's father do business together. Kicks and the Limp sometimes even see each other at adult parties though they never talk. All Kicks could expect is to be held, cursed at a bit, maybe have his hair mussed or his clothes rumpled, but that's probably it.

We turn to Scaler.

'Move quick,' he says. 'Lay low. Don't let them catch you alone. We have to find a safe place till this blows.'

The bell rings, we run where the crowd is thickest and file back to the classroom. We avoid eye contact with the Limp. When the bell rings for lunch, we do as Scaler says and move quick and lay low. The Limp and his gang tail us but as long as we stay where the crowds are, the best he can do is taunt.

'What'd we do? What'd we do?' Tri squeals at him during lunch, from a safe distance but with a full mouth. The cafeteria monitor tells Tri to sit down and keep quiet.

'You know what you did,' the Limp answers and some of the beasts point down. We can't rely on the crowds forever.

When dismissal comes, we move fast again and hide behind the building of the school's maintenance staff. We get a few shouts from the carpenters and plumbers that we're not allowed there, but we're not doing anything but standing around, and they don't feel like chasing us off, so we stay until it's safe to leave and go home.

The next day I reach school early, before anyone else, and find our safe place.

It's an old room near some seldom-used stairs and fairly far from everything. It's locked, but I know locks and locks know me, so I am able to open it with a bit of paper clip coaxing. It used to be the developing room for the old photography club, and it smells like it: old chemicals, film, and developing fluid. It's dusty and dark even with the lights on, and it's full of rusty tools, discarded iron bars, and planks of old wood, but it's out-of-sight, and more than enough for four. I whisper to Scaler during our first class. We move fast again at the recess bell and we take many turns and twists to throw the Limp off before disappearing into the room. The guys like it.

We hide there again after lunch and do the same at dismissal. The next day's more of the same but the Limp doesn't let us forget.

'We'll find you,' he whispers to me and Tri in class.

'What'd we do?' Tri squeals again.

They get Tri two days later during the lunch break. After eating we move fast out of the cafeteria but Tri gets left behind, taking a twist when he should've taken a turn. He ends up out in the open just when one of the beasts rounds the corner beside where he is and grabs him, then drags him back into the darkness of an empty corridor and to some unknown place.

We never make it to the safe place. You know what they say: you don't have to outrun the lions, it's good enough to not be the slowest. We watch from afar, we hear Tri's screams briefly before one of the beasts clamps a hammy hand over his mouth, and then he's gone.

Some hall monitors see Tri's legs sticking out of a dirty corner behind some cabinets just before the start of the first class after lunch. They carry him past our classroom, rushing to the clinic like there is no tomorrow, and for Tri, maybe there isn't. He's trailing blood. The Limp and his beasts are experts. They look clean and innocent. Not a drop on them.

At dismissal there is no need to rush or to go to the room. The school is hot. All the hall monitors are on alert. They shake down a lot of guys, even the Limp and his beasts, but they deny everything and nobody speaks up against them, not us, no one.

The next morning, Tri doesn't come in. We all hear from the teacher that he'll be away for a while. She tells us the name of the hospital and the room number in case anyone wants to visit. The principal makes an announcement over the intercom, something about discipline, an investigation, and expulsion, but Scaler, Kicks, and I don't hear any of it. I turn to the Limp and he sees me, points down, and my dread rises for real this time. This is no game, not any more, if it ever was.

Days pass and nobody gets caught or expelled, which means Tri hasn't said anything, that is if he can say anything at all. Things cool off as they always do, eventually, and we know that it is time to get back to the room.

And we don't know how it happens or why, but we're rushing and running after the dismissal bell, and with all that's happened to Tri our panic and our terror is really alive now, and we're taking our twists and our turns and we reach the room and run in and shut the door behind us, and the Limp and his beasts are already in there, waiting.

'Hey,' he grimaces, or smiles, and we scream, but they stop us like they did with Tri and cover our mouths with their hands.

But whoever's got me hasn't grabbed me that well. He covers only half my mouth, and his fingers are there, and I let myself go, I let it go, I let it go completely because I don't want to end up like Tri, bleeding and in pain and in the hospital and afraid to talk. I don't want to be afraid any more because it's crap to be afraid all the time, so I bite the beast's finger, I clamp down like there's no tomorrow, and I know there won't be a tomorrow for me or for Scaler or for Kicks if I don't bite down like I was really sick and tired of being afraid over something we didn't do. It's funny but with that finger in my mouth my thinking clears up and it strikes me right then and there that maybe we really didn't do anything, there was no need for the Limp and his beasts to have us do anything, because it's enough for him that we are simply there.

I bite and I gnaw and I grind my jaws and his screams fill the room and I feel and hear something crack and snap and I'm hoping it isn't my teeth. I taste something metallic on my tongue and I'm hoping it's the beast's blood and not mine but whoever's blood it is it's a good thing because the metallic taste reminds me of the old, rusting iron bars on the floor. They're perfect, just perfect, so I dive and grab one and I swing and swing and the room is dark even with the lights on and I see only dancing shadows and I'm shouting as I make fleshy contact with my iron bar on stupid beasts, so many stupid beasts. I hate, hate, hate these beasts.

I feel hits too, some on my side, some on my head, and each time I ignore them and strike right back in the same direction with my iron bar. The strikes are sometimes thuds and sometimes squishy but they all feel great, they all feel fantastic, and there's still a lot of screaming and shouting and crashing and crying but I don't let up and I swing my iron bar. I want there to be a tomorrow for me and for Scaler and for Kicks even if it's too late for Tri and let there be no tomorrows for the Limp and his beasts.

Then someone pushes me and I fall and I wriggle and I scream with all my strength because my iron bar is ripped from me. Whoever's pushed me is big, so big, bigger and heavier even than the Limp, and my struggling does nothing this time. He drags me out, away from our room, out into the light and I'm still screaming, but now that there isn't too much crashing and shouting around me I can hear myself: 'That's for Tri! That's for Tri!' and I don't want to end up like him, please, oh please not like him.

A hall monitor has got me, got his arms wrapped around me, but I'm still screaming, and he's shushing me, but I don't care and shout some more. I see Scaler and Kicks are already out of the room and standing beside some teachers and they look okay but I'm not sure because they've got some blood on them too and they're looking at me like they don't know me and I still don't care. I see some other teachers walk out the room and one of them is leading the Limp, who's got a hand to his eye and there's blood trickling through his fingers, and he's holding his leg and limping badly. The Limp is limping, haha! I realize I don't know why he's called the Limp in the first place. Even some of his beasts, they're being supported by teachers because they're big and we're not and they've got blood all over them too. I don't see all of them being carried out, so that means some of them are still in there, maybe down, and that's good because it's all for Scaler and for Kicks and for me and for Tri, oh God what have they done to you Tri. I'm not afraid any more and I'm still shouting, and I know I've got tomorrows and those beasts don't, haha! And I'm damn glad that I let it go, let it go at last. It feels so good when you finally let it all go.

The Sparrows of Climaco Avenue

Late in the afternoon, as the steel-framed derricks on the skyscraper summits hoisted their cargoes of cement and iron on cables as thick as a man's leg, the sound of a large gong echoed over all, resounding from the farthest horizon, where the sun-washed sky met water.

Pre-programmed, the cranes continued to lift their consignments up, storey after storey, grinding and squeaking against their cogs and pulleys, but the builders and every other person in the city stopped. All eyes turned to the empty ocean.

The gong sounded for a second time, then for a third, each time louder, and the last brought palms to ears and teeth to grit. Above the water and against the distant clouds, a speck appeared, approached, grew. When near enough to manifest as a large, fast-moving black mass, everyone stared up with wide, unbelieving eyes.

More than a mile long and a mile wide, a cloud of sparrows flew into the city; the loud fluttering disturbed all hearts that heard it.

For centuries there had been no verified sightings of birds of any kind, and many did not know what to make of these creatures. None of the people knew what to call them; neither the crones nor the wizened were old enough to recall that time when prophets walked the earth and warned of this moment before disappearing in despair. In the centuries it had taken for this day to arrive, all belief had been whittled bit-by-bit to forgetfulness.

The flock circled the city, and where its shadow fell people cringed and hid. Parents brought their children indoors—to the dismay of these young ones, who alone pointed at the sky with smiles and laughter on their lips.

Television and newspaper reporters came out in droves; photographers aimed their cameras upward and took thousands of pictures; the police and the army brandished their weapons, waiting for orders, ready to fire; scientists cupped their chins in their hands and pondered the meaning of the sparrows' flight and appearance, as did sociologists, historians, writers, poets, artists, musicians, and false soothsayers.

The preachers and clerics were taken by surprise with the sudden upsurge of devotees who entered their holy places, pleased for the sermons and homilies that suddenly needed to be heard. They researched dusty, ancient books for words of prophecy, explanation, punishment, or hope, long unsaid and unread, each to their own creed's interpretation, none of which was the same.

The sparrows flew for half an hour before settling on Climaco Avenue, the city's highest point, where the buildings were tallest—hundreds upon hundreds of storeys high, and still rising—and where the most prominent of the city's citizens lived. The sparrows landed, roosting on ledges and windows, and on the many cables and phone lines that hovered over the streets like an intricate spider's web. They blanketed everything in a square mile, and the people in that place immediately evacuated. The builders were instructed by the authorities to remain where they were and to continue their work; but none followed and they fled to the ground.

The mayor was not pleased. He had been forced to leave the luxurious City Hall on Climaco, and was incensed that his orders for all construction to continue could not be carried out. In the sudden, unimaginable absence of noise, he realized how much pleasure he took from the clanging of hammers and the growl of pneumatic drills that had constantly drifted down from above.

Stalemate, he thought, *but not for long.* He told his nephew, an army lieutenant, that he planned to retake his office with the younger man's help.

'By force, sir?' the young lieutenant said, his voice quivering. He and the other soldiers had been taught to use their arms only against other men; as a younger military student, he faintly remembered reading about the never-ending war in a land over and beyond the horizon, from where the creatures had flown. He tried his best not to show it, but to the lieutenant they were terrifying and unnatural; nothing should be able to soar through the air as they did. The mayor felt the same misgivings, but jaded with age, he ignored them.

'We'll use force if need be,' the mayor said, his jaw set. 'What weapons would be most effective?'

'Perhaps the flame-throwers, sir?' the lieutenant answered. 'But we might burn something we shouldn't.'

'Bah. We can rebuild.' The mayor puffed his chest outward, then as an afterthought, concluded, 'We'll issue a warning, of course.'

But his bravado failed when, for the fourth time, just as the sun started to set, the gong echoed once more from across the sea. All the sparrows raised their wings in time to the sound, but did not take flight. Beneath the streets and the buildings, the ground groaned and shuddered, then, inexplicably, began to sink.

As the waters flowed over the land, overwhelming the docks and quays, dousing all the street and lower-level lights, people screamed and ran into the buildings, ascending in an attempt to escape the inrush. A few thought themselves wiser and made for the ships along the shoreline, but the earth beneath their feet sank far too quickly and the water engulfed them before they could approach any vessel. The funnelling waves pushed the boats inward, inland, to dash and sink them all against the buildings by the waterfront. Those by the sea were the first to die.

Trying to ignore, though still fearing the sparrows, people poured into the buildings that lined Climaco, filling them to overflowing. Every available space inside every structure on Climaco was crammed body to body. From there, the survivors watched the waters flood the city's lower levels.

The mayor took refuge at the top of the tallest building, almost three-hundred storeys up; the building still had power, but this did not last. As the city sank, the sea retook the lower lands and eventually reached Climaco. When the building's basements— which housed the generators—became inundated, the lights sputtered and went out.

The buildings sank, a slowly diminishing skyline. Even from far below, the mayor could hear the screams of the drowning. The people in the lower floors fought and clawed for the pinnacles against those above, forcibly removing the smaller, the weaker— either trampling them down or hurling them out the windows and into the sea.

The sparrows took flight each time the waters rose to reach them, settling on every available ledge and sill, always staying just above the waters.

When at last the city was engulfed, and all were either dead or dying, the sparrows took flight again. They circled the space where the city used to stand until their strength waned and gave out. As one, the birds fell, to drown as the people before them had. Many bodies sank, but many stayed afloat, among them the mayor's and the young lieutenant's. When the sun rose the next day to light that piece of the world, corpses bobbed for miles around. It took days for the current to disperse them all outward and away, and longer for the marine predators to consume them. When the last body sank, every trace of man, bird, and city was erased.

Cherry Clubbing

Hey! Hey!

Francis? You're . . . Frank, right?

It's me, Richard! We met in Bangkok some years back. We joined that private beach-tour group to Thailand together.

Smooth sand, clear water, blue skies? Tropical sunshine to die for? Ring anything? No? Heh. Can't blame you for pretending. We've got to be careful nowadays, but there's no need to be coy with me. I *know* you.

You really don't remember? Heh, sure. Okay, I'll play.

I was the one who lost his balance and fell off the boat when our group went off to chase dolphins. You had to come back and get me, remember? We lost the dolphins after that. I probably scared them away. Everybody got pissed at me.

Yeah! Yeah, me! That's right! I'm Dicky, Frank! Good to see you! Geez, you weren't shitting! You *really* didn't remember me! So how've you been?

Me? I'm fine. A little bit more flesh around the pate, a bit more of a paunch, but never been better. I'm still up to my old tricks. Same ol', same ol'. And you? Same too, huh? Busy as ever, like bees, that's us.

Hey, man, you got time? I'm not doing anything right now, just hanging around, looking. You, same? People like us, we're always looking. Let's park our asses somewhere and catch up, what do you say? Guys with our 'shared interests' don't get to jaw often, so this is a special occasion!

Hmm . . . this is a pretty big mall. Open air, too. Smells funky without air-conditioning, but that's the way it is here. You know another thing about the Philippines? Their beer is excellent. San Miguel, they call it. Saint Michael, in English. Heavenly when chilled. Let's get a couple of brews, my treat.

Come on, let's try that place. It looks cheap, good, and clean. So does the waitress. They don't hire our 'types' here, but she still looks like she hasn't developed yet. Perfect for the both of us.

But nah. We're just 'reading the menu', 'kay? Here, grab that table. We're not 'ordering'. I want to make that crystal clear. Let's just say that we shouldn't do dirty things in this backyard. Here, as with most places, it's either 'to go' or forget it. It's funny, for some reason they say 'take out' instead of 'to go' in this country. Anyway, we shouldn't send out any smoke, if you know what I mean. I'll tell you why later. Special reason. Trust me, it'll be worth your while.

That got your full attention, didn't it? I knew it would. Anyway, later.

Two San Miguels, babe. No, not the light stuff, the ones in the brown bottles. Yeah, the Pale Pilsens. And hey, cutie, you sure you're over? Aww, don't give me that look. I'm sure you're fine. Just sayin', that's all. You're cute, you know, and sexy. You're *fresh*. That's a compliment!.

See, she's smiling! It's *in* them, Frank. It's *in* them, I tell you, like it's in us. I don't know why only we can see it and the rest of the world can't.

Aww . . . I'm sure she understands English, c'mon! Maybe she doesn't get everything, but this is the Philippines, baby! They speak English well enough. Funny-sounding, but fine. They love Hollywood here! To them, anyone from where we come from is a fucking movie star!

Even with our 'shared interests' I didn't expect to bump into you. What're you doing here? Hell, I mean I *know* what you're here for, same thing as I am, but a classy someone like you runs in different circles than I do. If not for that Thailand tour, I doubt we'd have ever met. What're you *technically* here for? Trade convention, huh? Buying the native handicrafts? Cool. No? Boring? Hey, sorry, man. Then you're lucky you got away for some time off.

Alone? Sucks. Your company's running on the cheap, sending their best man halfway around the globe without help. But that's just the way we like it, eh? And you're not alone any more. You've got me!

Thanks, girlie! Here's the cash, with a little something extra for you. Keep the change. Remember me kindly when I come back. And I *will* be back. For *you*. I promise.

See? See? She's still smiling. Love her dimples. Drink up, pal. Good, eh?

Don't you just love the pointiness of their ears? Makes their eyes bigger, doll-like. So sweet, especially when they're at just that right height. They're perfect that way. That's how you started out, I'll bet. That's how I did. Hell, that's how we all did. We started with one of them pointy-ears, then there was no turning back, and it was on to greater things. Better things.

It's fate, Frank. Fate. There's a reason we met today, here of all places. You're looking, I know, 'coz that's the way it is. Those like us, we're always looking.

What happened to who? Scarface? Oh, you mean Ronald! You remember him? Hey! Why'd you remember Ron but not me? Oh, his scar. That's right, he had that scar down his cheek, that's why the nickname. Of course, stupid me. Evil-looking cut, made him look like a crook, but he was the complete opposite. As big and as strong as a bull, but what a great guy. The best. He was a good friend.

Yeah, 'was'. Got caught, he did. Sad. Shit happens, even to the best of us. How'd it happen? Long story, but we've got time. You ready for a long listen?

Ron and I had been travelling together for years, even before Thailand. They finally got him about two years ago when we were in Cambodia. And of all things, he got caught with some pointy-ears. Yeah, just the pointy-ears, same as that waitress, nothing more, but enough to bring everything down on his head. What a way to go. He was with several of those elves, in fact. It was his own damn fault, really. I like to say it was bad luck, but Ron, he was the reckless type. He always was. Once the mood hits him, he forgets to be careful and just goes for it. Shoot from the hips, full speed ahead, damn the torpedoes. He even forgets to lock the door sometimes. It's not good to be that way. It's never good. You always got to keep some kind of control going until you're sure you're safe and alone.

Scarface . . . Ron . . . was living on borrowed time. The only reason he lasted as long as he did was because of me. I was the one watching his back, making sure we did things safely, that we didn't rush. It was his fault, I know that, but I sometimes blame myself for what happened. What if I had been there that night to watch his back as always, instead of sick in bed with the flu? He'd be here with us now, that's how it would've played out. But I couldn't lift myself out of bed back then, and the dumbass couldn't keep himself inside. He followed his hormones and just had to go and do it without checking that all was clear. I warned him to play it safe, to make sure that everything was clean. I knew he wouldn't listen though, and there was nothing I could do. 'Yeah, sure,' he had said, then smiled at me, closed the door to our room and left me alone with my virus. Those were the last words I ever heard him say.

The next time I saw him it was on TV. Bad, real bad. They showed the full raid on prime-time news. A raid! Yeah, I can smell your fear right now. I can see you sweating. A fucking raid. There must've been a dozen warning signs but Ron walked right into it blind.

I still remember exactly how I felt when I found out. It was a few hours after Ron left. My fever had gone down and I was thinking of going out after him. I switched on the TV for some noise—it was almost uncomfortably quiet—and the news came through. I froze and nearly puked when I heard the reporter say, 'We are broadcasting a live raid here from Svay Pak, Phnom Penh.' Ron was headed there. He had been eyeing a group of pointy-ears the night before, fresh from the provinces.

It's our worst nightmare. I watched it unfold right there on the TV, and I couldn't wake up because it was all real. I remember how the screen shook as the cameraman followed the policemen up the narrow wooden stairs to the 'safe-rooms' behind the bar and restaurant. I remember the heavy pounding of their running feet; they banged on the door twice then kicked it open. Ron got caught red-handed in the full glare of the lights. His eyes were large and white when he turned to face the camera. I can still see the shocked expression on his face. His scar stood out like a black shadow, and with his long hair plastered to his head with sweat and blood he looked like some kind of pirate. He was holding his favourite riding crop, the brown one—you remember it from Thailand, don't you? Yeah, that one—he was holding his crop up in mid-stroke, about to bring it down again. He was licking blood off his other hand at the same time.

Everything stopped. I swear, no one moved and everything became quiet, like hitting the pause button except I could still hear the whimpers and the moans in the background. Then someone off-cam swore like a sailor and it was like a signal to act. The camera shook again, followed by more cursing, shouting, and crying. The screen blurred. I could hear Ron's screams through it all. I heard breaking glass, falling furniture, and whacking. A lot of whacking.

When the TV cleared, Ron was crouching on the floor. His hands were cuffed behind his back. Someone pulled his head by his hair and showed his face to the camera. One eye was half-closed, puffed, and it looked like his mouth and his ears were bleeding. A policeman spat in his face, and another kicked him and he fell and hit his head with a sick thud. 'Let him know what it feels like to be on the other end of the stick,' someone said.

They panned the camera to show the elves on the bed. There were five of them, two boys, three girls, naked as a brand-new sunrise and fucking beautiful. Clearly our 'types', all of them. Man, if Ron was reckless, he made up for it with his energy. Terrific work. He's the only one I knew who could do five at a time in one go, and then be ready for five more not an hour later. And he knew how to work them, work them hard and work them well. Ron did a great job. They were gorgeous.

Of course the damn cameraman played it up for all it was worth. Sensationalism rates, that's the law of media in any country. He showed close-ups of their bare backs and chests, their tight butts, their legs, their faces. I loved the way they looked into the camera, the lights glowing in their wide eyes. The tear streaks on their faces were precious, and their sniffling and whimpers turned me on, in spite of everything. Ron, he raised these lovely, long, criss-crossing welts all over their hard, tight, little bodies. So red with blood, so angry. I ran my hands over the TV screen and I could almost feel the bumps. Mmm.

This is how I think the story went down: Our dumb friend leaves me and he forgets everything except for the fun he's going to have. He heads straight for Svay Pak, probably pays the cabbie double to run the red lights and get him there quick. He has the cab stop right in front of the bar and he gets down. He doesn't tell the driver to stop some blocks away so he can walk and check the area out like we've always done. Any new cars around? Anybody who may be watching the place? Hiding in the shadows? Nope. He just walks in all excited and big and goes directly to the boss and asks in a voice as loud as he is tall for the elves he met the night before. The bosses, they never know anything either. It's all money-money-money to them. They're more reckless than Ron. If I was a boss . . . well, later. So, Ron, he's told to go out back to one of the rooms and to wait there, and he does. Then the boss brings in the elves. None of them know that it's all a set-up. The news crew and the police have been waiting, they've probably seen the whole thing from their unmarked cars parked outside. Or maybe it's their man inside who sees Ron walk in the bar, sees him talk to the boss, sees him go out back. Then he sends a signal— tips his hat or something while sitting by the window—and the cops and the crew move in and it's all over.

When Ron left me that night, I prayed hard that nothing would go wrong. The percentages were on our side, after all. What are the stats? Ninety-nine times out of a hundred, nothing happens right? Ninety-nine times out of a hundred you're left alone and you get to do what you want as long as you've got the cash. That's my personal rule number two: always have enough cash, because if you've got enough you not only get to do what you want, but if something goes wrong, you can always pay your way out with no questions asked. *No problema.* But there's no way you can pay your way out of a live TV camera in your face. Not enough cash in the world for that.

What's my number one rule? Well, it's two rules in one, my friend. It's that important. Always, always play it safe, and leave no trace, ever. Better that than sorry. Keep my rules to heart, you hear? I'd hate to see you go down like Ron.

The newscaster ended her report by calling us criminals and monsters that needed to be hunted down and brought to justice. That chick, she just didn't get it early enough, otherwise she'd loosen up and know what it's all about. She'd love it the way we do. You and I know better. There are more of us out there every day, and I'm sure that one day we can all come out and not have to worry any more.

And it's not like we're hurting anyone, right? I mean, these elves and those like them, they live forever! They just go on and on and we, we're old and our years are numbered, but they'll still be around. Nothing hurts them, or if it does, they've got years and years and years to get over it. We don't. Their whole lives are ahead of them, and they love it. It's in them, and we . . . we need this. It's in us as much as it's in them.

I beat it out of there faster than a bolt of lightning, flu or no flu. Spent the night at the airport shivering in a jacket. Took the first available flight out to somewhere, I can't even remember where. I played it safe. I couldn't risk Ron not ratting me out, not with what I knew the police had in store for him. Poor guy.

Aww, shit, Frank. Reliving all this is painful. I miss Ron. He was great to be with. Why'd he have to go and be all stupid?

Remember what he did in Thailand? On the beach that night when the fishermen brought in their fresh catch of mermaids and merlads for us? Remember what he did? Yeah, you do. Haha! I'm glad you remember. I'm glad I've got someone to share that memory with. That idiot really couldn't control himself. Heh. Careful there. You're snorting beer through your nose. Heh.

The night was so clear, the moonlight and starlight were so bright on the water when the fishermen came, do you remember? What time was it? Midnight? No? You're right, that's too early. Maybe two or three in the morning. I can still see their boat gliding through the waves. I can still hear the crunch when it hit the sand and they pulled it up onto the beach.

The lead fisherman came to me first. The old guy reached into the boat and he lifted out a bundle wrapped in wet canvas. The bundle was wriggling when he brought it to me. The fisherman grinned as he pulled the canvas aside and revealed the most delightful sight. My first mermaid, you know, my very first. She looked up at my face and I could see the stars reflected in her eyes. Her hair was stringy and long and I pulled it aside so I could see her small, precious breasts. Exquisite, my friend.

You got a merlad, you say? Golden scales on the tail? Whoah! You lucky bastard! Well, we were all lucky, weren't we? That tour was expensive but worth every cent.

Ron, that bastard, haha! He couldn't wait for his catch to be brought to him. He ran up to the boat, reached in and lifted two bundles up all by himself. Carried them under each arm, walked to the nearest stretch of open sand, threw them down, pulled off the canvases and went at them with his crop, his fists, his elbows, his knees, and his teeth like there was no tomorrow. The sounds they made were intoxicating.

That broke the spell for all of us, didn't it? I brought my mermaid to the space beside Ron, pulled off my belt, and began to do my thing. The rest of you were all over the boat like sharks in a frenzy. Massive, man, massive. Our cries and theirs were crazy wonderful, all around us, all over the beach. Shit. Loved the way they mixed with the sound of the surf. I got off real good, more than thrice, I think. Best group action I've ever had, hands down. Haven't experienced anything like it since. Gawd, we all needed to help each other back to the huts before the break of dawn. I couldn't walk straight. My body was that sore. Ron had that goofy smile on his face too. What? Me too? No kidding? Haha! Then you too!

Haha! Oh my, good times, those were. *Great* times. We need more of those. Oh my. Oh my my my my. Sometimes it's really worth it to be alive.

Hey, hey, which brings me to this. I'm about done with my beer. Are you? Good, hey, I think it's time I share with you my little secret. Bend over closer, will you?

Heh. I'm a boss now. Yeah, well, one of them. I have some partners. Been here in the Philippines for a bit more than a year, and my job is to bring people like you, who don't have a clue in this country, to where you want to be.

We've got everything. Elves, mermaids, nymphs, satyrs, dryads, you name your type we have them. They have different names for them here, but it's all the same, it's all good, and I can do the translation for you. You want to go wing-pluck some sprites and fairies as a teaser? I can show you where. You want a dwarf, or a satyr or two, either with full beards or shaved smooth, just let me know. Since we're old friends, you get yours at a special rate, the wholesale rate. I guarantee you it's all safe and hidden. You know how I work. The rules, man, the rules. You won't have to worry.

I've sampled all the merchandise, one of the perks of being a boss, and they're wonderful here in this country. The local varieties of the elves and nymphs and what have you, man, they're great! And there are a lot of them. There's a different taste to them, too. Delicious! Exotic! This place is a goldmine, a fucking paradise, I tell you.

Come here, get closer.

It's so wonderful here, we were able to find something extra special.

Angels.

Yeah, you heard me right. Our stars. The demand for them is high. We got lucky, found them, and caught them. Pretty easy. You take anyone or anything by surprise and it's all easy. You want seraphim? We've got them. You should see—no, *feel*—what they can do with their wings. It's nothing like you've ever felt before, I promise you. And their blood, flows like liquid light and tastes like rainbows.

You know what? We have cherubim, too. No kidding. Yeah, I know. Hard to believe, eh? We've got them. We're the first in this part of the world to have them. I tried one of them cherries myself. A nice, plump, rosy-cheeked one. Beautiful dark-brown curls. Oh, wow. Heaven. You should try one. Highly recommended.

Elves and mermaids sound like old car engines coughing exhaust compared to an angel when it sings. If we could set up some mass action like we did in Thailand, I'll bet we could experience an entire choir. It's the heavenly host treatment, baby!

I hope you're feeling strong. These angels, they may have smaller bodies and slighter builds, but they're twice what any elf or dwarf is made of. Takes a lot just to hold them down, and a lot more to get them to sing. I doubt if even Ron could take more than two of them at a time. His riding crop would be useless.

You need something heavier and harder, but the effort's worth it, believe you me. Me? I took an aluminium baseball bat to mine. Needed two hands, too, like a caveman with his club. Some of my customers prefer crowbars. But I think a stiff plank of wood would be fine, as long as the wood is the tough kind and you've got strong enough arms. Yeah, wood is good if you want to, you know, savour it. To make it last longer. If you've got the endurance, go with wood!

So, you want to give it a try? I can take you to our place right now. Like I said, wholesale price for you, pal. You high-rolling, jet-setting executives have got all the cash, anyway. What do you say?

Great! Let's finish up. Fate, Frank. It's fate. We were meant to meet here today. Bet you had no clue where to go before you met me. Bet you were just taking your chances.

Ahh, that San Miguel beer is sweet, as sweet as cherry blood. *Almost*.

Hey, girlie! Thanks for the beer! Remember me, and remember what I said. I keep my promises. I'll be back for you.

Smiling. They're *always* smiling. Damn gorgeous. I swear I'll never get tired of them.

Come on! Let's go get you some cherry!

A Boy and His Bat

My new neighbours were a source of bafflement for me.

Oh, of course, from the outside they looked highly respectable. They were the best-looking of families, the kind whose photograph would look good on top of a piano. There was the father, Mr Paulo del Rosario; his wife, Tillie; and their only son, Kevin. They were a well-to-do, well-bred, family— decent, friendly, and very amiable. Their being newcomers to the neighbourhood did not mean a thing. After just a few days of living in the newly constructed house right beside mine, they blended into the neighbourhood as perfectly as the right amounts of coffee, sugar, and cream in hot water.

What first raised my eyebrows was the behaviour of their son. No, please do not jump to the conclusion that I spy on my neighbours out of the debasing instinct of curiosity bred by malice. That kind of person I am not. But the window of my workroom, on the second floor of my house, overlooked my new neighbour's garden, which was also Kevin's playground. I remembered my childhood, and envied Kevin for not having to queue up at the slide or wait for the bigger boys to finish playing in the sandbox. Mr and Mrs del Rosario loved their eight-year-old only just enough to spare no expense in lavishing him with the best toys, swings, slides, and games. I am quite sure that Kevin's room was filled with these toys, since every now and then I saw him playing with a matchbox car, or a robot-doll, or with soldier figurines.

* * *

A fortnight had not yet passed when I saw Kevin in his personal playground brandishing a heavy aluminium baseball bat. The way I saw him use it stirred the beginning of my curiosity with the new family next door, a curiosity that, I am embarrassed to say, led to many hours of intense observation. I wasted a lot of time in my workroom and no matter how much I rationalized, in my heart I knew I was simply eavesdropping. Yet, in spite of my guilt at invading other people's privacy, I could not tear my senses away from the events that transpired in the del Rosario household. It happened like this:

While working on the accounting ledgers of my little store in the city, I was interrupted by a horrible, rhythmic clanging. It was the sound of metal striking sharply against metal. It was as loud as it was irritating, and it came from next door. Since I could not continue my calculations because of the noise, I stood up from my desk and walked to the window, already mentally phoning Mrs del Rosario to ask her to correct whatever was wrong with her plumbing fixtures, her car, and whatnot. But I stopped when I reached the window, for the clanging came not from some mechanical failure, but from Kevin. He was banging his aluminium bat against the slide's steel ladder.

I did not know what was going on in young Kevin's mind, but it certainly must have been vicious; vicious enough to set him to swinging that heavy bat over and over against the ladder. But the expression on his face did not betray any sign of a temper tantrum, something young boys are prone to when they are frustrated. Instead, he was grinning widely like a madman, seeming to enjoy every ear-jarring sound he made. I did not think that a small boy

such as Kevin could repeatedly swing a heavy bat over and over
again, but he kept at his little game with the vigour and consistency
that only the interest of young children can sustain.

I had completely forgotten about my books or about calling
Mrs del Rosario. I didn't know how to tell her, in a sane and polite
manner, that her son was 'banging his bat on the steel ladder of
his slide'; courtesy, as well as plain curiosity, and even a degree
of incredulity, dictated otherwise. So, with dumbfounded interest,
I watched the fascinating scene.

For the next three or four minutes, he swung the bat against
the ladder. Strangely enough, I was the only observer who was
attracted to the noise. No one else inquired, no one on the street
stopped and craned their neck to look futilely beyond the tall walls,
no one rang the doorbell to ask what the matter was. He made
noise loud enough to awaken his great, great, grandfather from
the peace, but the living were dead to the ruckus. Only after these
three or four minutes had passed did one of the del Rosario maids
shout at Kevin from within the house for him to stop. When he
refused, she came out the back door huffing and puffing to wrench
the bat from the boy's hands and drag him, crying and complaining
at the sudden termination of his little sport, into the house.

Well, that's the end of that, I thought to myself, and I primed
my eyes and ears in anticipation of seeing and hearing Kevin
being scolded by his mother and father for being so naughty. But
nothing happened for an hour, two hours, three . . . and I went
back to my ledgers during the restored tranquillity.

When I stood up from my desk again, this time to stretch
my legs, I took a passing glance outside the window. There, on
my neighbour's terrace, which was just off the playground, I saw
Mrs del Rosario clearly berating and scolding, not Kevin, but
the maid, in an animated and heated fashion. For the second
time that afternoon my eyes widened, this time more in shock
than surprise. I am sure anyone would have expected Kevin

to be punished for his deed and the maid duly thanked. Yet the opposite had happened. The poor girl could only lower her head in front of her mistress while Kevin, that pitiful scoundrel, clung tearfully to his mother's knees.

* * *

Kevin certainly used his bat again because the next day, after I had seen Mr del Rosario leave for work and his wife step out—to shop for groceries I assumed—there was a dreadful crashing and tinkling, thudding and whacking, that emanated from within my neighbour's house. I myself was just preparing to go to work, but once more I was overwhelmed with a degrading inquisitiveness, and I rushed to my workroom window.

The noise continued for a few moments longer, and then ended when Kevin rushed out the back door and into his playground, desperately being chased by all the maids. He was still wielding his aluminium bat. When he reached the Jungle Jim, he turned around, faced his pursuers and, with venom in his voice, shouted, 'I'll tell Mommy and Daddy! I'll tell Mommy and Daddy!' and swung his bat dangerously around his head. The maids stopped in their tracks and pleaded with their young master, but it was clear that Kevin adamantly wished to be left alone. They could do nothing but retreat into the house and watch with fright as the young boy resumed his game of whacking his bat against the steel ladder of the slide.

I had seen enough, so I left the window and went to the store where I could concentrate and focus, but my work still took a drastic hit in quality and performance.

* * *

I could not escape the next incident as well, for it happened in the afternoon of the very same day. It was the most intensely violent act Kevin had performed yet. Thankfully, I was not present as an audience to have watched him wield his bat again, but I pieced the events together from the clues left behind from the boy's latest destructive mood.

When I arrived home from work, all was quiet, both in my lot and in the house next door. I went to my workroom and I looked out the window at Kevin's playground again. I assumed that Mrs del Rosario had, in the morning, gone to do the grocery shopping. It seemed, though, from the evidence, that in addition to the groceries, she had stopped by the pet store to buy a puppy for Kevin. In the playground were things that a boy needed to care for his dog. There was a typical, mass-produced dog house, a leash draped over its roof, a mat, a dog's supper dish, and a rubber bone.

Of course, I thought. Kevin was lonely, and that explained his violent moods. A dog, a companion, would be perfect for him. It would give him something to love and care for. What's more, I envisioned an even more complete family than before, for what could look more perfect in a family portrait than a mother and father with their young son hugging an adorable, frisky puppy?

My eyes scanned the yard, looking for Kevin's new pet. When I saw it, however, I turned my back quickly, for there, right under the set of swings, was a mass of brown fur and blood. The dog's collar was still around its neck, but even in the quick glance I took I saw that it had been pulled too tight and had choked the animal. Leaning on the lightly swaying swing was the bat, stained red.

Thoroughly sickened, both at my voyeurism and at the scene, I left the house again in search of the company of comforting friends.

* * *

What is the measure of our involvement into the lives of our fellow men? Are we our brothers' keepers, or will our nosy perusing into others' lives, no matter how well-intentioned, only create the division and conflict between neighbours that I, in my personality and make-up, try so hard to avoid? Notwithstanding my incomplete musings on this, here is, on instinct, what I immediately thought about the matter:

Would that I had done something the moment I first saw Kevin wield his bat. I had observed a distressing malady in its infantile stages, and I am quite sure that I, as an outside party, could have done something that the people involved could not. Perhaps I could have prevented it from becoming as distressing as it did. I am neither a psychologist nor a sociologist, but I gleaned instinctively that there was something crooked and awry with the love Mr and Mrs del Rosario had for their son, as well as with the love Kevin had for them. The unlucky maids would easily get over the wounds of living in such a house, but the three members of the del Rosario family were the biggest casualties.

Barely three weeks after the incident with the puppy, the del Rosario's moved out. Ever since that day I never saw Kevin, or his bat, again. I tried to make subtle inquiries, but Mr and Mrs del Rosario had closed themselves off, no longer neighbourly, no longer blending in. Instead, they cleverly avoided answering my questions. After they moved, I worried, and I do still worry, about Kevin constantly. I wondered why I would, but I can only point to my weak personality as a feeble excuse. Yet I dream of seeing him happy and content one day when he is older. If my courtesy and embarrassment had not held me back, I would have perhaps found the courage to hint lightly to the del Rosarios that there are better ways of loving their son. I have sworn to myself that the moment the perfect opportunity presents itself, if and when it ever does, I would take it.

But perfect opportunities never come, and up to now, since the time they departed, I have yet to see any sign of the del

Rosarios. They left no forwarding address, and I fear the growing certainty that they are forever gone from my life.

My eyes may never set on that family again, and I do not know whether to feel blessed or cursed.

The Concierto of Señor Lorenzo

The *kalesa* halted right in front of my humble boarding house. I folded my newspaper and looked up from behind the front desk, just as the sound of the horse's canter on the cobbled street ceased. The early afternoon sunlight, as bright as my lobby was dim, caused me to squint to get a better look at the two people disembarking from the upper carriage. All I could see were their silhouettes framed in the doorway.

The driver hefted the baggage down; a blur of action. He lifted them through the entrance and, without stepping inside, placed them on the lobby floor. He then held his palm out— strangely, at a full arm's length—to the other one, the passenger. It struck me then that the driver seemed to be in a rush and that he was crouched and breathing heavily from exertion, even if the bags he had just carried did not seem particularly large or heavy. The passenger picked from a purse and delicately placed some coins into the open hand. Perhaps it was a trick of the light on my eyes, but the scene froze and the two silhouettes became shadows, dark and thin, almost skeletal, the taller one holding out some benediction to the other, more shrivelled one. It lasted but a moment. In the next, the horse on the street whinnied nervously and shook its mane, restoring movement. The driver took his money and bowed, then quickly clambered onto his box-seat; with a click of his tongue and a 'Hee-ya!', the kalesa clopped away.

The remaining man approached the front desk slowly, his footsteps echoing hollowly. As my eyes adjusted and my vision cleared, allowing the silhouette before me to gain features, I noticed his mouth: wide with two long lines of pinkish lips in a pale face, open in a grin that seemed to show more than the normal amount of square, white teeth.

'Good afternoon,' he said, his tone friendly but his voice rasping. 'I would like to rent a room. May I?'

I grunted an affirmation, opened the registry between us heavily, and waved lightly at the pen. He took it and I noticed how pale his hands were, and how long and thin his fingers. He bent over, dipped the pen in the inkwell and signed his name. 'Edilberto Rosalino Alhambra Lorenzo' was his name, or so he had written. It was a name typical in length and the usual pretension of the upper classes and those trying to be like them.

'Señor Lorenzo,' I addressed him, but even so, I was unsure of his name's claim to any inner *kastilaloy* heritage; though he perhaps could pass, I wasn't convinced of any strong Spanish blood in him. There seemed an oddness to his look, not quite *mestizo*, but not quite *indio*, either; and in the first place, my boarding house was not one for my 'betters'. Nevertheless, his manner and bearing were impeccably societal and as long as his money was good . . .

'I would like to have a room on the highest floor, away from everyone else. From the outside, I noticed a high corner protruding on one side of your fine establishment. Could that be an attic, perhaps? An upper-level mezzanine? If that is indeed a room, I saw that the window points to the sky, to the stars. That would be perfect for my needs.'

This was the most he had said in one breath and I admit to having been taken aback. The upper-crusts never bothered with more than what needed to be said to those like myself. He must have noticed my surprise, but instead of holding back as I expected, as someone of his stature should've done, he pressed on, still loquacious.

'I am, ah, an amateur musician, you see, a student in between teachers, if you will.' He waved his arm toward his baggage and

I wondered how I could have missed the bruised and faded guitar case between two other smaller pieces of luggage that were equally battered.

'I would not like to be a disturbance to your other guests.' He doffed his hat, revealing a bald, bulbous, white pate bulging with purple veins. In doing so, he aged himself instantly by twenty years before my eyes. For a moment, he seemed less human and for the first time, my unease threatened to overwhelm me; I shuddered from a cold that came from within. No, he was not young, only seemed to be when properly concealed.

'You see,' he continued, 'I am working on a piece of music, a short *concierto* and an even shorter opera, just an amateur's attempt at art, so to speak. I expect to be composing late into the night and I would not like to be a disturbance to your guests.' This time, at the sight of his teeth and his strange smile, I was nearly unnerved.

'It's our most expensive room.' Business was just so-so and my occupancy was not high, but for some reason, I uttered the words as if to dissuade him. My voice quivered slightly as I spoke and I struggled to regain some control of my illogical nervousness. He asked for the rate and I named one higher than normal, which he accepted by re-opening his purse, counting out a wad of bills and placing them neatly before me.

I could only cast my eyes downward at the money, mumble a 'Yes', and ring the small bell I keep behind the reception table. Rosalino, the teenager I employed as an all-around assistant, walked in from the back.

'Lino,' I said, acutely aware that I was making an effort not to directly address my new guest, 'here are the keys. Show Señor Lorenzo to the high corner room. It is his for the next four nights. Take his bags.'

'Be careful with them,' Señor Lorenzo said, turning his smile onto the boy. Lino hesitated and his eyes widened, before he hurriedly picked up the bags and trotted up the narrow wooden staircase on his bare feet.

Señor Lorenzo nodded to me, restored his hat to his head, and followed Lino upstairs. For some reason, to my ears, his footsteps echoed more hollowly than Lino's muted thudding.

* * *

'Did you hear him last night, Señor Santos?' Lino asked me the next morning. We were both early risers, and were sharing a breakfast of eggs, garlic rice or *sinangag*, and Barako coffee.

I had heard the faint plucking of guitar strings from my quarters on the ground, but only when I strained to listen. They were easy to ignore and not loud enough to disturb me. My own room is hidden away behind thick walls and a thick door, and I am not in the habit of sleeping by an open window, even with a *kulambo*—an old but still serviceable mosquito net. When I sleep, I prefer it to be quiet and utterly dark.

I remembered then that Lino had chosen a recess at the back of my boarding house as his place of rest, needing only a makeshift wooden cot, a rattan *banig* to lie on, and one of my discarded *kulambo* for protection from insects. That spot was three stories down and directly below the window to our latest guest's room. If anyone would have heard Señor Lorenzo's music, it would have been Lino.

'No, I did not,' I told him. 'Did you? Was he any good?'

'Oh, he sounded like a good guitarist, Señor . . .' His voice trailed off and I noticed immediately the way the young boy's face scrunched up in perturbation.

'What is it?' I asked.

'It's not that he played poorly. I could hear much of his music. He's certainly a better guitarist than my Tito Manuel from Pampanga. Tito Manuel has been playing all his life, but Señor Lorenzo is far more skilled. It's just that . . .'

'Yes?'

'Señor, I could not recognize the type of music he was playing last night. It did not sound like any music I have ever heard before. It was different.'

'Did you enjoy his music?'

'No, I can't say that I did, yet I couldn't stop listening. Even if his music made me feel—what is the word?—"uncomfortable", I wanted to hear more of it. But our guest did not play his song through. He would stop, then resume again, then stop, change something a bit in the tune, as if he did not yet know fully the song he was playing.'

'He did say that he was composing a *concierto* and an opera.'

'Perhaps that is why.' Lino sighed. 'I could not sleep at all, Señor. Strangely, I did not want to sleep, and I felt irritated whenever he would pause. I'm sure I did not get more than three or four hours of rest last night.'

'Was he up that late?' I asked. It was then that I noticed how bloodshot Lino's eyes were. 'Well, this cannot be. You cannot do all the work I need you to do if you are not rested. Maybe we can move you to one of the small closets in the meantime. You can empty one of them of whatever they contain and move in temporarily.'

'No!' Lino surprised me with the passion of his response, with the way he jerked his head up at me to express his dismay at my suggestion. He reacted as if I had meant some punishment for him, when clearly, I did not.

'No, sir!' he said. 'I'll be fine. I can still do my work and more, if necessary. I am happy where I am!'

'Well, then . . .' I began, when the sound of someone clearing his throat startled the two of us out of our conversation.

Señor Lorenzo stood in the doorway of our small kitchen. We had not heard him approach, not even the creak of the stairs as his weight pressed on the wooden steps. He was, as far as I could tell, wearing the same clothes as the day before, and when he said

'Good morning' and smiled at us, the same, initial fear renewed itself within me.

'I hope I am not bothering you,' he said, 'but I will be going out today and I will not return till later this evening. I have locked the door to my room and I would like to request that it not be disturbed. I am quite particular about my belongings.'

It was a strange request. Did he not want us to sweep the floor, or empty his bedpan, at the least? But I could only nod my head at him.

'Will you be playing again tonight, Señor?' Lino asked with a boyish eagerness that surprised me as much as the audacity he displayed in addressing a stranger he should not have been speaking to in the first place.

'Yes, and for every night,' our guest said. 'Could you hear me? I am sorry . . .'

'No. It's all right,' Lino cut him off, another breach. 'It's all right, Señor.'

'Well, thank you. Goodbye.' He turned around and disappeared out the main door.

I would have reprimanded Lino then and there for speaking before being spoken to; I would have reminded him that only I am allowed to speak with guests and if he is ever questioned, he should answer quickly and directly without developing any familiarity. But just as Señor Lorenzo left, someone else thundered down the stairs.

Another one of our guests, a Señor Juan Martin Fernandez, one of two travellers from Cavite, all dishevelled and wild-eyed, burst in upon us.

'Carlito is dead!' he screamed.

Lino and I followed him upstairs to their shared room. He was gibbering about how he had woken up from a poor night's sleep haunted by terrible dreams and when he stepped over to his companion's bunk to shake him awake, he discovered him with eyes open but blank, staring at the ceiling, his mouth open and frothing with green sputum, his face a ghostly pale and lined with thin, purple veins.

I sent Lino to call the *Guardia Civil*, and he returned with them and one of their superior commanders post-haste. They all reached the same and immediate verdict that I had: one of our guests had died in his sleep and a cart was needed to take his corpse away.

* * *

The worst that could happen to my business was a fire. A fire can destroy everything and leave you with nothing. It is said that it is better to be burgled than to have your home and your business go up in smoke and flames. But a death! Unlike with a fire, I still had my building, but a death at this moment felt just as devastating.

The doctors came and took the body away. One of their assistants clicked his tongue as he covered my guest's face with a white sheet. They saved me from the indignity of being questioned, instead turning their curiosities upon Señor Fernandez. While he was whisked away, I heard the word 'quarantine' uttered more than a few times. Memories were still fresh as we were only four years removed from a flu that had ravaged Manila.

My other guests had woken to the commotion. From the corners of my eyes, I caught them whispering among themselves. They saw and heard the same things I had. In a few minutes they were all dressed and lined up at the reception. I entreated them to stay by telling them that nothing had been conclusively proven, that it was all speculation, but to no avail.

'We don't know anything yet,' I pleaded. The more polite guests apologized, the ruder ones claimed that their past night was restless and that their dreams were disturbed, as if that could have been my fault. By eleven, they had all packed, paid, and left, all covering their mouths with damp handkerchiefs.

I could only wait for the authorities to return, either with the news that they were closing us down or that my boarding house was clear.

'Señor Santos?' Lino called me from the stairs. The tremor in his voice betrayed his fear.

'What? What is it?'

'I think you should see this,' he said and he led me upstairs.

I thought he would lead me to the room where our guest had died, to show me some frightening piece of evidence that indeed, the flu, or some other plague, had returned. But he turned away at the landing and brought me instead to the high corner room. The door stood ajar.

'Did you unlock it?' I asked. He nodded and handed me the master key I trusted him with.

'I thought to clean his room . . .'

'No, you did not!' I said, with all vehemence and he knew I spoke the truth. Chastised, he bowed his head.

'I wanted to see his things. I wanted to hear Señor Lorenzo's song again.'

And now, so did I. What could have taken a hold of this boy, who previously had shown no taste for any kind of art, to make him obsess over this music?

I faced a choice then. To shut the door and lock it, to keep myself in blissful ignorance, would have won me over, if not for Lino's plea.

'You must see!' he said, and he pushed the door wide. He took my arm and pulled me bodily into the room. The assault on my senses was immediate.

My grandfather suffered from vertigo late in his life and he always complained about losing his sense of balance, of dizziness. This was how he died—he fell down while getting up from the sofa in the *sala* and the sudden movement caused him to fall and hit his head on the floor. He never woke up from his coma. The doctors couldn't do anything and neither could the *albularyos* with all their herbs and potions. When I entered Señor Lorenzo's room, I knew that this must've been how he felt.

Tacked on the walls were large, yellowing parchments of hand-drawn illustrations of what seemed to be buildings, but none of a kind that I had ever seen. In my youth, before my family fell on difficult times, I had been to Europe, to Paris, Bonn, Stuttgart, London, Barcelona, Madrid, Berlin. They were fascinating places and I had thought then that I had seen the apex of human architectural creativity. Upon seeing these drawings, I knew then that this was something beyond man's capabilities. Taken together, the drawings presented a city designed following some inhuman geometry, one that seemed off compared to the world I knew. The angles made no sense and neither did the placements of what I took to be gables, awnings, and other fixtures. My eyes began to tear up, which was fortunate because I knew that if I stared at the drawings for too long, I would surely pass out. And these were simply pencilled sketches! I feared for what this might do to me if they had been real.

'Señor!'

Lino's voice called me back and I shielded my eyes from the walls so as to focus on him. I reached out and held his shoulder for support. 'Look,' he said and against my will, I beheld the crumpled paper he thrust in my face. My schooling had included some formal lessons in guitar, an instrument which I had no talent for, but I recognized the writings as sheet music. The piece was untitled, and I noticed in parentheses a German name, Erich Zann, but surely our guest was the true composer behind it. Beneath the notes were words, lyrics, I presumed, of his opera, but it was in a language I could not recognize—and based on the formations of the letters—much less pronounce. On the table was an open, leather-bound book, handwritten and not printed, ragged around the edges, with many loose sheets of music and other notes inserted between the pages. I recognized some of the words from this book as being the same as those on the sheet Lino held up to me. Clearly, they were being transcribed to the music.

As with breakfast earlier that morning, the sound of a throat clearing made us look up and as before, standing in the doorway watching us with unveiled rage, stood Edilberto Rosalino Alhambra Lorenzo.

'I warned you most politely,' he snarled, 'not to enter my room!'

'Señor! It was me! I am sorry!'

'Wait!' I said, mustering my authority. I was still the proprietor of the boarding house and I called on those rights. Despite my quivering knees, I said, 'We have had a death due to illness this morning, sir, and the doctors and inspectors may shut us down. I am expecting them to return any moment. We only inspected the room to make certain of its safety. You may have to leave at once. These are unusual circumstances!'

In his silence, Señor Lorenzo was more menacing than he would have been in passionate anger. He stepped inside the room and closed the door behind him. Lino and I were frozen in place and could only watch. He stepped slowly to the unused bed where, for the first time, I saw his guitar case lying open. He sat on the bed and pulled his guitar out and in the strangest of reactions to all that had happened, began to play and sing.

Lino's mouth opened wide in surprise and recognition; the song was surely the same as the one he had played the night before. Señor Lorenzo started slow, calling forth mixes of chords and sounds both weird and dreadful. Certainly, the music was not natural to this world, and I could hardly believe the indefinable vibrations that he was calling forth from his throat and from his instrument. It filled me with a brooding sense of wonder and frightening mystery. That such a symphony could be brought forth by one man playing one instrument was unbelievable.

The music picked up and Señor Lorenzo's hands and fingers began to move in such a frenzy that they became a blur to my eyes. He began to shriek his words in time to his playing and as if in answer, the sky outside clouded over and the wind began to howl through the open window. Señor Lorenzo was certainly a genius and also clearly insane—his eyes took on a look of madness as he turned the full energy of his work upon us. My heart beat rapidly in my breast.

There came a choking sound beside me and Lino fell, grabbing my shirt as he did so. His eyes had rolled up into his forehead and his mouth frothed with saliva and mucus in mimicry of the dead guest from the room below. I am ashamed to say that I could not help myself, and in disgust and repulsion, I stepped back and detached myself from my assistant's clutching hands. Then, in the most unbelievable of events in a morning filled with them, I perceived the sound of another voice, one that growled in guttural anger, and another kind of music akin and in answer to Señor Lorenzo's play, descend from the dark sky outside, growing in volume in its seeming approach. I ran out the door, fleeing for my life.

* * *

I do not remember staggering down the narrow staircase. I do not remember rushing outside as fast as I could in an attempt to distance myself from the madness that nonetheless seemed to follow me wherever I went. I do not remember finding myself in the middle of the cobbled *calle*, the kalesa bearing down on me from out of nowhere, the horse's whinny, its rearing forelegs, the screams of the driver and bystanders.

* * *

I came to my senses in the hospital. My legs were broken, as was my right forearm. The doctors and nurses were kind, if wary.

A young orderly, more patient than the rest, explained that I had woken screaming many times in the middle of the night, calling out my assistant's name and the name Lorenzo, then laughing maniacally before falling back into unconsciousness. For three nights, I had been this way and they had needed to move me to a separate room because of the disturbance I was creating for the other patients.

I inquired as to my boarding house and Lino, explaining who he was to me. I gave my address and the name of my business to the orderly, which puzzled him, but he was accommodating enough to agree to send someone to check. He told me later that the messenger he had sent reported no such edifice at the site, claiming to have found only a vacant, grassy lot.

I think now: would that I could do the same for my memory and lose it as I have lost my boarding house, because in my dreams, in the darkest of nights, I can still hear the cacophony of Señor Lorenzo's music; I can still hear his voice scream a babel of words whose meanings were never meant to be comprehended by man. When I am deepest in recollection, the world I know slowly transforms into that city, shaping itself into its mad architecture. In those moments, I know where I need to go to find my home; to find Lino, if he is still alive, which I doubt; and Señor Lorenzo, whom I hope to never see again.

Storm Song

I

She is the moon, they are the stars. The moon and the stars were formed with the world and before the world, and their light is far older still.

The moon sees the world below from her place in the heavens, alongside the sickle, the bear, the crab, and the twins. On this night, they see the city in its false glory. The light the city gives is a poor, poor imitation of their own, and though the city does not know it—will not admit it even if she could—the moon and the stars know that unlike their light, its light cannot last. Though the city's light lasts for a thousand, thousand years, it cannot last like theirs.

They see that the city's finite twinkling will dim soon. From the east come clouds of grey. The grey storm clouds come, inexorable, creeping in over the world's seas, and the city does not see them. She may know that they come, but she does not see them. The moon and the stars, think to themselves: the city's lights could be dimmed by such a simple thing, the storm.

II

He is the storm. The storm is air and water. He is wind and rain.

In cold he is made fertile, in warmth he is conceived. In a twisting cycle he is birthed over its manger, the sea, and is clothed quickly with the damp and the chill, howling in his bed with new-birthed rage and fury.

The storms are nothing if not constantly reborn. They have been many, an army, a multitude. They are all siblings, come all from the same blood. They wrap themselves in the same howling wreath that shreds the sky with tendrils of jagged light and the crack and cacophony of the bellowing firmament.

He is air and water. He is wind and rain. He is clouds and vapour.

He is the storm.

The storm nears the city.

III

She is the city. The city blinks and twinkles in the quiet night, unmoving but alive. Deep in her bowels there lies unease, a sense that this night will be unlike others, that this night will not stay silent. Perhaps, in her deepest recesses, she knows of what slowly creeps her way. But the city is proud, and will never admit to her vulnerability.

Or perhaps, she chooses not to.

Some of her inhabitants share the city's deep unease, and sleep fitfully, if at all. Restless, they toss and turn, or stumble about in the dark and half-dark, moving between shadows with apprehensive expectation.

The city lives. She blinks and twinkles in the night. With all its living, she tries to sleep.

IV

They are the living. The living breathe in places high and low, above the streets and on the streets, and beneath. They breathe in beds and in cots, on roads and corners, in alleys and doorways. They breathe in chairs and at tables. They breathe by lamp posts, trees, and walls. They are awake and are asleep, and they breathe by themselves or in each others' arms, alone or entwined.

Of those who sleep, the living dream of many things. Each of their dreams is but a fragment of the one mystery they all belong to. Yet, they are unaware of this, believing in themselves alone, as absolutes. Tonight, they will soon share the storm as they share their common mystery.

The living are young. The living are old. The living breathe. They inhale air that is uncommonly still this night.

V

He is the night. The night is a cloak of layers of shadows, each deeper and darker than the one before. He wraps himself around stone and rock, bark and steel, as easily as around hope and imagination.

The night is quiet. The night is patient. He waits. Even if it takes the length of the centuries or the length of minutes, he waits. It is all the same to him, because he is the night. He is the end.

The night, wrapped around the city in his infinite patience, waits for the storm.

And then, the night is no longer quiet. The storm is here.

VI

He is the storm. The storm is a whirling lash, he is a furious whip. He snaps and bursts upon the city, and scars her with lines of wet welts.

The storm laughs, cackling and crackling, revelling in his wild turbulence. He is bliss. He is joy.

With countless thongs, bladed and razored, he flays and thrashes about in a frenzy, laying waste till the city's flesh is left raw and torn open, bleeding from his finest slices.

The storm's voice booms and explodes as he works his art. Guttural and deep, his song is a cacophony of exultation, of glee. He sings his passion to the city, an ardour he cannot hold back, and which the city cannot contain. There is too much of the storm's fervour for the city to hold, too much of his undulating waves. Beneath his vehemence, the city breaks.

He is the storm. The storm cycles around the city and pours forth his zeal and turmoil, spending himself in spinning wave upon spinning wave. He lays low the living, and brings forth the dead.

VII

They are the dead. The dead are wet. The dead are filthy. They scatter like the city's finest litter, in patterns haphazard in symmetry. With their unmoving stillness, they display forms and angles—natural and unnatural, elegant and clumsy. Against fences, on streets and under streets, in alleys and doorways, by lamp posts, trees, and walls, the dead lean or lie, while the storm pummels its torment on them and on the city.

The dead still dare to dream, and in their dreams they speak. Together, they say: 'Why?'

'Why?'

An echo of reverberating hollow voices that have lost their breath. They say it, over and over again, for any of the still-living to hear. And those still-living will hear them. The living will one day hear the dead. There is no answer to their question.

The dead still dare to ask. The dead still dare to dream. It is all they have left.

The dead are young. The dead are old. The dead do not breathe. They no longer need to.

There are some dead that still move, floating in the currents, bobbing on the crests and troughs of the storm's floods.

VIII

They are the floods. The floods are the children of the storm. They gather and grow; they feast on the city. They creep through her like the tendrils of trees but faster, filling her streets, turning them into tributaries of themselves, pooling into her plazas and walkways. They find the city's living, they find their homes. The floods fill the living, replacing their warmth with the storm's dank and the storm's chill.

The floods are hungry. The floods are greedy. Their grasp is ice. They take all that can be taken. They reach out and pull the breath of the living into themselves.

They are the floods. They grow over the city. They grow into the city.

IX

She is the city. The city is cold. The storm has left her, lifting his weight from her, up and away. Her shivers are deep tremors that all those within her feel to their bones. She no longer twinkles and blinks in the night, a night that is also no longer quiet. Deep in her bowels, the storm has sown the remnants of his violence. The darkness is pierced by the wails and screams of those still living. But the city is still proud, and will never admit her vulnerability.

Even if she is laid low and to waste, even when cracked and split into two by the storm, even when her light is extinguished, and she now knows what the moon and the stars know—that her light cannot last, that she cannot last—she will never say so.

The moon and the stars may not know how it will be so, but they know this for truth: that not only for the city, but for them all, the only true end lies with the night.

X

She is the moon, they are the stars. The moon and the stars have been part of the night for as far as they remember, far older than the world, as old as their light. When they became aware of their light, the night was there.

This is the truth they know: we are all a part of the night, and the night is the end. Be it storm or city, flood or wind, living or dead, the moon or the stars, in all things there comes an end. After all things, there will come the night. Yet, until that end, we continue.

The moon and the stars wish to share this truth with the city, with the living, with the dead, for it is a comfort to them. But they do not know if their voices are heard. They do not know if the city, the living, and the dead are listening. But the moon and the stars will tell this truth through the ages, with hope for their understanding.

He is the night. The night is patient. He waits. Even if it takes the length of the centuries or the length of minutes, he waits. It is all the same to him, because he is the night. He is the end.

XI

She is the dawn. The dawn breaks over the city.
She lights the day with all that it could be.

A Sampaguita Breeze

Marivic was only three when Lola died. A first-generation 'water baby', she was born right after the first rise of the seas that took the coastal areas of the country, including Manila Bay near Roxas Boulevard. The bay broke its shoreline and swept through, up to the Malate and Intramuros area, drowning all the history, all the heritage of old Philippines.

After that, there were two more major inundations, all within two years—the second coincided with Lola's passing while pushing their family inland as the seawaters rose into Metro Manila proper. The third drove them to the highest elevation points in the city, which found them in Quezon City, near the University of the Philippines (UP) campus.

Stories reached their family that the coast now marked Timog Avenue, with the waves lapping up against EDSA, lining the city's main thoroughfare. Their family settled near the open grasslands between the UP campus and Katipunan Avenue, but beyond that, there was news that the Barangka area had become a deep swampland. They were an island now. In fact, the whole city had become a series of islands with their own population of refugees, with the taller edifices from Pasig, Makati, and Taguig poking up out of the water like the fingers of drowning men reaching for air.

By the time Marivic reached the age where memories could settle, she only knew a world of houses on stilts, boats, and rafts; of insects that swarmed from the water across whatever dry land they could find; of the constant sound of lapping waves and the humid moisture in the air; of crowds compacted onto whatever square metre of soil they could hem their way into; and always, the mixture of smells—human, animal, and marine—combining together till the scent of fresh air became an experience rarely enjoyed.

MARIVIC

Their house, a shanty, a ramshackle hammering of wooden beams and flooring, creaked as the currents below pushed the stilts to and fro. Small splashes on the roughly cemented wall they built the stilts against added to the chorus. Early evening had settled, but it was mostly dark already, as energy was given only for the most essential lights.

To protect their hands and arms from splinters, her mother, Rita, had wrapped their small kitchen table with paper torn from old books gathered from an abandoned warehouse. Her mother, a former teacher, had taught her to read, and she had memorized some of the sentences from the pages on her side of the table, pages she could not help but see at every meal. Though she could not understand all that she had read, she understood and memorized this one: 'A normal sleep breathing cycle is about 3 to 5 seconds, and the inspiration/expiration phase duration has a range of 0.3 to 1 second.'

So, ten-year-old Marivic pretended to sleep. She slowed her breathing and counted four seconds between breaths to make it look as real as possible. She felt her chest heave upwards with each intake of air, and hoped it looked convincing enough to anyone who might be looking; though she was truly performing for an audience of one, Rita, her mother. She could sense her mother's body beside her, restless, shifting constantly to find a comfortable position for her own slumber. Marivic stayed patient and waited for her mother to become still.

Marivic was afraid that in the pretending, she might actually fall asleep, and fought hard to stay awake while maintaining her slow breathing. But she didn't dare make her move too soon. She wanted her mother to get some rest.

To stay awake, she focused on two things: the slowly dwindling noise of the world outside, and Lola's promise.

Every Christmas, when it is quiet at night, make your way to a clear place, where the air is free and the wind can reach you, and from wherever I am, I will send you the scent of sampaguitas on a breeze. I have nothing else to give you. I am broken, poor, and old, but I can leave the memory of sampaguitas to you so you can remember something of what we were before the waters rose.

'She died soon after,' her mother had told her. 'We buried her in the Manila North cemetery, in a small *nitso* on the third floor of steel structure 9 in the farthest corner from the street. The waters rose even more some months after, and she's underwater now. Probably forever.'

That first Christmas after Lola died, Marivic's mother carried her to an open, quiet space and waited for a clean breeze to make their way to them.

'There it is!' her mother eventually said. 'Can you smell it? It's the scent of Lola's sampaguitas! She has sent it to us, just like she promised! Can you smell the sampaguitas, Marivic?'

Marivic thought she did. And every Christmas since then, she believed that the pleasant scent of jasmine she caught a whiff of was Lola's sampaguitas each time.

Marivic fought her sleepiness and waited. When she believed she heard the even breathing of her mother, she turned her head slowly and slitted her eyes. In the gloom, she could see her mother had turned her back to her. The rise of her torso was steady.

Marivic rolled off their hard bedding ever so slowly, dropped to the floor, landing like a cat, before tiptoeing off.

She did not see her mother sit up and turn.

'Do you promise to be careful?' her mother said.

'I didn't want to wake you,' Marivic sighed.

'I would have woken you before midnight if you had really fallen asleep,' her mother said. 'Be careful, yes?'

'Yes.'

'I could go with you.'

'Ma, you know you can't.'

'I know. I just needed to say that. Say a prayer to Lola.'

'I will. Go back to sleep. I'll be back soon.' Marivic disappeared through the doorway.

PABLO

The trail of blood led up the makeshift, rickety, wooden stairs, over the water. Luckily, no rain had fallen yet to wash the trail away.

The blood is not yet dry. He's about half an hour away.

Sheathed and hooked on his belt, Pablo favoured the jungle knife's handle in his left hand and thumbed the edges of the brass knuckles in his right. He took a deep breath before stepping off of dry land and up the stairs, to the maze of wooden shanties that had been built over the water.

The smell of humanity was always worse over the water. That's what happens when you pack as many people as you could into as limited a space as possible. With not even basic plumbing available, with only the water below to dump human excrement, it was like living over a septic tank. It hit him like a permeable wall, but it didn't take him long to get used to it; he'd spent too many of the early years over the water to soon forget what it was like. The monsoons and typhoons had not yet come to wash away the filth, if not the structures, too, but it is easier to rebuild over water than it is to acquire liveable space on land. Land was for the privileged.

It was stiflingly hot under the mix of galvanized and corrugated roofing supported only by old wooden beams. Pablo weaved his way over the rickety boards like a cat, alternately crossing through shadows and light. When the waters had risen, he had been the first to adapt, having been a seaman in a past life. The water did not bother him as much as it did the perennially landed. Walking over wooden planks, which swayed from the undulating water below and caved in slightly with each footstep, was no different than walking on a lilting ship. He followed the trail of blood, noting that the distance between the droplets on the planks shrank the deeper he made his way into the shanty community.

He did not pass many people as he followed the trail. The few he saw were half-hiding behind corners, walls, and doorways, respectfully keeping their distance. A rushing, wounded man clearly seeking escape was always followed by imminent danger. He was that imminent danger, and he counted on their prudence to mind their own business and stay alive.

When the distance between the drops of blood shortened, he knew he was close and slowed to a creep. The trail led around a corner, across a narrow walkway in the open air, over greenish-brown stagnant water, and through a doorway into a corner hovel. There was just that one entrance, no other exits. In the sunshine and over the filth, Pablo crossed the walkway slowly, through the doorway, and into the darkness of the hovel.

The mid-afternoon sunlight streamed through a small window onto the wall at the far end, illuminating the face and chest of a body slumped against the wall. A pool of blood had collected on the floor around it, but he could see that the chest still rose and fell with every breath.

'You shouldn't have taken what wasn't yours, Carlos,' Pablo said, his hands squeezing into fists around the handle of his knife and his brass knuckles.

Pablo stepped closer and saw that his mark was done for. The wounds he had dealt had been enough; it was only a matter of time. He relaxed his fists and squatted down to eye level.

'We are what we are, *pare.*' Carlos' voice was raspy.

Pablo slipped his knife back into the sheath on his belt and fished out his phone from the holder beside it. He needed a picture, maybe even a video, as evidence for his boss. He aimed, focused. Carlos smiled.

Smiled.

His instincts didn't warn him soon enough. He let his guard down too soon. He didn't check his surroundings. He was overconfident. He was stupid. He felt something sharp sink into the flesh between his neck and shoulder.

His attacker pushed him from behind and he fell forward. He felt another stab into his lower back that took the wind from his lungs. His strength allowed him to kick up with his legs and push off from the floor, shaking his attacker off, who was light, wiry, but fast. When he turned to reach behind him, he grasped at air.

A small and wiry silhouette stood out briefly against the door. From his height, he couldn't have been more than fifteen. The light was behind him, so Pablo couldn't see his features, but Pablo found himself fixating on the large shock of hair around his head that took the light like a halo.

'Go!' Carlos said, and the silhouette was gone.

An ambush. I'm so stupid.

Pablo tried to rise, but a weight on his shoulder pushed him back to the floor. Carlos had pulled himself to his tormentor and used his body to keep him down.

'Maybe we die together, eh?' Carlos said. In his hand was another blade, ready to fall.

But Pablo still had enough strength to twist his torso and bring his fist with the brass knuckles around for one solid punch to Carlos' head. Carlos did not move any more after that.

The effort had torn his shoulder wound wider, causing more of his blood to spill out and mix with that of Carlos', but he was more worried about the stab on his back, wondering if the blade had punctured anything vital.

Pablo staggered to his feet and stumbled through the door to the sunlight and open air. He was still alone; the boy was nowhere to be seen. He leaned against the thin railing beside the walkway and tried to draw deep breaths, even though the air was fetid. He felt like gagging.

A soft, cool wind blew from somewhere, and he couldn't believe it, but through the stench, he caught the aroma of sampaguitas, the flowers whose jasmine scent could not be found anywhere any more.

He had lost track of the days; he didn't know it was Christmas. He remembered his mother, and unearthed memories of family came to him, like water washing away the earth to reveal a hidden city below. He had a sister, and a niece he had only met twice before he became too ashamed to go back to them. The memories were better than his current life, and a sense of devastating loss overcame him. He slumped down to the walkway and into his own darkness.

EMMA

It used to be cool. We didn't sweat like this before.

Emma looked wistfully up at the air-conditioning vents on the ceiling. Centralized, they were long disused when the many powerplants became submerged; sometimes, at night, she could hear scurrying sounds from the vents.

When electricity became scarce with fewer working power plants, all the regular people were given just enough for low-consumption needs like lights and basic communications. The country had stayed with cheaper coal, investing only in a few solar and wind technologies. That power now was reserved only for the powerful.

Only the monsoons brought any break to the relentless tropical heat.

'Do you have breaktime coming?' Alfonso approached and asked, his voice muffled through both his surgical mask and his protective headgear. Alfonso was one of the few doctors still willing and able to work.

She focused on pulling the syringe out of her patient's shoulder and swabbing it properly before nodding her head and showing five fingers. *In five minutes.*

'Forget it,' Alfonso said. 'We're being called to the top.'

Her eyes widened.

'Yes, the penthouse,' he said. 'Finish up, bring your medical kit, then come with me.'

She had never been to the upper stories of the building, which was formerly a hospital. The lower four stories were inundated, the next four were converted for utilities and logistics: water transport, washing, sorting, food preparation. The next ones above were the living quarters and community spaces, open to all. She considered herself lucky that she was a registered nurse and physical therapist—*registered to what, now that the Department of Health is underwater?* she often asked herself—as it allowed her access to the middle stories just below the highest three.

'Hurry up,' Alfonso said. 'Let's not keep them, any of them, waiting.'

Emma had been given a small room there as her living quarters, with a nearby bathroom shared with only ten other healthcare workers, all with the same benefits. Meals were brought to them from below and they were guaranteed these luxuries as long as they never stopped working and took care of the people brought to them. With a good six hundred people in the building at any point in time, half of whom were patients, this semi-privacy was, indeed, welcome.

She taped her patient up, told him to press on the bandage for a few minutes then hurried after Alfonso. She didn't want to lose any of her benefits.

Doctor Alfonso was walking fast, almost jogging. As a doctor, he had it even better than Emma. Bigger rooms, less people to share a bathroom with.

'Do you know what this is about?' she said, breathless.

'No details,' Alfonso said. 'But obviously, when we're called, someone up there, someone important, must really be sick. Come on, let's not waste time.'

Time. She had lost track of how much time had passed since she had become a permanent resident of the former Metro Manila General Hospital. When she had finally found time to make a rough guess, she came up with, what was to her, a staggering period: three years, eight months, and three weeks. She hadn't left MMGH for so long. She hadn't seen or talked to anyone else except her co-habitants. She hadn't even seen family.

She kept long hours at work just so she could take her mind off her family: her sister, her brother, her niece. How were they now?

Alfonso led the way past the non-functioning elevator bays and through the open fire escape doors. Emma could not see his face clearly through his protective mask, but she was sure Alfonso was smiling as he told her to 'Take a deep breath' before trotting up the stairwell. She swore under her breath and followed him as fast as she could, mentally counting down the twelve floors to the penthouse.

Halfway up she was heaving and pulling herself up by the banister, but she was still relatively fit for her age and knew she could take the climb. She took some smug pleasure that she beat him by a floor to the top, where a burly security guard garbed in all-black—even his surgical face mask—awaited them.

Both of them were breathing heavily and sweating profusely, but that didn't bother the guard as he scanned their IDs and asked them to remove their masks so he could see their faces. Once he was satisfied, he whispered 'OK' into his radio and opened the door.

The first thing Emma felt was the cold. Comfortable, comforting cold. Air conditioning!

They have air conditioning on the penthouse! Well . . . of course they would.

She could tell they were just in an anteroom, but she noticed the paintings right away. And after the paintings, she noticed the designer furniture, elaborate chairs, tables, and shelves. Then she noticed the décor and the elaborate fixtures and stood there in unmoving shock. It had been too long since she had seen anything that wasn't functional and spartan. Before her eyes was a picture from a lost past, and though she could admire the beauty, she could only think about what a waste it was given all the basic human needs that went unmet every day.

Then she noticed the smell, or rather, the lack of it. Even on the lower floors, the awful stench of Manila found its way through. It was inescapable except . . . here.

'Air filters,' Alfonso said, reading her mind and nodding at a large, grilled contraption hanging from the ceiling.

'Move,' said a curt voice from behind her, from another big man in black, one she hadn't noticed.

She and Alfonso followed the order and scampered forward. Still breathing hard, they were hastily herded through rooms they didn't know still existed in their world: a living room, two separate kitchens, a dining area. A library! Through open doors they caught brief glimpses of other rooms that could have been a game room, a den, a playroom, a guest room. Emma couldn't help wondering how many bathrooms there were, and how many—or few—they had access to.

They were ushered deeper in, down a carpeted corridor where the lights were dimmed until they reached the farthest door at the end and were waved inside.

It was a relatively small room, a child's room, and the child inside, a young boy, lay sleeping on a small bed. Unblanketed and in a thin sleeveless shirt and shorts, the skin on his arms, legs, neck, and face was dried, scaly, peeling, and in some places, bleeding. The flakes of his skin lay around his body on the sheets along with dark brown stains that looked like dried blood. Some kind of cream had been smeared all over him. His feet were socked and his hands were gloved and tied together at the wrists.

He had a really bad case of the 'hydro-rash'. Emma had seen cases just as bad, but mostly among those who were always in extreme close proximity of dirty water. It was a mutated and more virulent type of *erythema nodosum*—painful, reddish plaques and lesions that infected the subcutaneous fat through hair follicles. But how did this sheltered child get infected? He was as far away from any kind of contamination as anyone could get.

'What . . .' Alfonso blurted before he was cut off.

'We tied him up so he wouldn't scratch himself any more,' said a stylish woman in her thirties standing by a far, open window; the window was open despite the air conditioning. She was dressed in body-fitting athletic clothes, a soft towel draped around her shoulders. Alfonso and Emma could not help staring because her face was made up, something neither of them had seen for years. She took one more deep drag of a nearly spent cigarette held between her fingers and blew the smoke out the window, flicking the stub after it.

'How old is he, ma'am?' Emma found her voice, remembering her place in time.

'Seven, I think,' she responded. 'Or eight. And hard-headed. I told him not to scratch, and we put some of my moisturizing lotion on him to take away the itch, but when we woke up this morning, he had scratched himself to the bone, and so here we are. That lotion was expensive. What a waste.'

'It's a good thing he's sleeping, then . . .' Alfonso said.

'We dosed him with an antihistamine. He put up a fight, but we got enough down to put him to sleep.' Emma noticed the teaspoon, the glass of water, and the bottle of red syrup on the bedside table.

'How can he be fixed up?' the woman said. Emma noticed she didn't approach but stayed where she was.

Emma stepped up to the bed and laid her gloved hand on the boy's forehead. Even through the insulated rubber she could feel the heat.

'He's also running a fever. Have you taken his temperature? Do you know how he caught it?'

'That what you're here for, right?' the woman screamed, losing her composure. 'Get to work and find out! You'll stay here for as long as it takes to fix this!' She skirted the edges of the room staying as far away from the bed as she could, slamming the door behind her. Even through her own protective mask, Emma caught the whiff of cigarettes as she passed by.

'Who was she?' Emma said.

'Probably the wife of whoever powerful person stays here. Or maybe she's the powerful one. Does it matter?' Alfonso answered. He pulled up a chair and set his bag on it. 'She's probably the poor kid's mother, or sister, or tita, and she probably expects us to know who she is. You and I are old enough to know that things haven't changed even after the waters rose. They're in power. When they call us, they expect us to follow.'

He pointed a thermal scanner at the boy's forehead. '38.3. Low grade.'

'Ma'am? Sir?' A small, thin figure peeked out from a small side door, one that led to the bathroom. The figure held her hands together in front of her chest. 'I'm the helper here. What can I do, *po*?'

'What's your name? And what's the name of the patient?'

'Anna, po. That's Charlie.'

'Anna, I'm Emma, and this is Doctor Alfonso Santos. We need cold compresses. If you have cold water bottles in the refrigerator and some towels, please get them.'

'More than half the bottle of antihistamine is gone,' Alfonso said, shaking his head.

They worked without breaks, changing Charlie's clothes and sheets, wiping away the useless lotion, disinfecting his scratches.

He stirred a few times but did not wake. Anna tirelessly went back and forth from the room to get whatever was needed.

After a couple of hours, they rested. Charlie slept more peacefully. Anna had left, taking the soiled sheets and clothes to be laundered. Alfonso had sat himself on a small couch and closed his eyes while Emma stood motionless staring out the open window, which no one had closed.

Emma had forgotten the sensation of cold air mixed with warm that was blowing in. She closed her eyes, caught the scent of jasmine and thought, 'It's Christmas! Lola!'

She opened her eyes, but the whiff of sampaguita was gone, leaving as fast as it had come. She teared up, wondering about her sister, Rita, and her niece and goddaughter, Marivic.

RITA

Rita watched Marivic hasten away.

She feared for her, of course. Her heart would be in her throat until she returned, but Marivic was small, quick; if anyone could evade sight, it would be her.

Earlier in the day, they had made plans to go to the coastline for a few minutes to anticipate Lola's gift when news from the neighbourhood captains said there had been a knife fight. Two men had died, someone said, but that was nothing new. Someone was always dying, and knives were just one way to go. The shanty town was put on lockdown and everyone had to return to their places and stay put.

Rita had decided to wait till next year. Their small space, deep within the crowded darkness, was too far for any fresh air to reach them. It was a disappointment, to be sure, but she did not see any way for them to move to open spaces while the lockdown was in place.

She did not count on the depths of her daughter's disappointment.

When they turned back, realization came to the young girl that they would not be proceeding, and she dissolved into chest-heaving sobs and could not be consoled. Amidst the terrible human ugliness around them, her daughter's sadness broke Rita's heart.

They hurried back, the throng of those turned back thinning as the pathways and walkways narrowed with every twist and turn on the rough wooden planks.

By the time they returned, the afternoon had dwindled to twilight. Rita held Marivic, still sobbing, and wiped her tears away with a clean face towel.

'*Anak*, I know, I know. One year is too long, but I am sorry, we cannot go. Not this year. I cannot afford the fine if we are caught. And I cannot afford to be taken away.'

'We can try to sneak away to the edges when it's dark, Mama,' Marivic said between sobs.

'It's too risky, anak,' Rita said. 'I'm too big, old, and slow to sneak around like you.'

Like you.

In an instant, Rita, who held in memory an inundated world long gone that she, at least, had once had the blessing of living in, knew she could not begrudge her daughter this horribly miniscule blessing: a scent, the beautiful and fragrant scent of the sampaguita that she and so many Filipinos had taken for granted. The flower had been sold by barefoot children, cripples, and old, wrinkled women at every hot, smoky, and traffic-filled intersection of every Philippine city. These poor had relied on the pity of drivers and passengers who would give them lose change for stringed garlands of sampaguitas to hang on their rear-view mirrors so the air conditioning can blow the scent inside the cabin.

A glorified air freshener was all it was, and now, it was all they had in memory of a lost world.

'Let's eat, anak,' Rita said. 'Then let's sleep a bit. Then when it's really dark and everyone is quiet, you can go.'

The joy and excitement in her daughter's face nearly caused Rita's own heart to burst.

'But, Mama, what about you?'

'It is all right,' Rita said with a wry smile. 'Just promise me you will be careful, that you won't let anyone see you, and that after you are done, you will come back to me.'

'Of course. I promise.'

Rita waited in the darkness, certain in her heart of her daughter's return, all the while holding hope that somehow, despite the stuffy, still air and the stagnant, stinking water beneath, Lola's gift would reach her, too.

Yet, even if it didn't, it would be all right. None of them deserved it, none of them deserved its memory. That Marivic could still experience it for those few seconds made her all the richer than everyone else in her generation.

MARIVIC

Marivic made her way like a cat in darkness. Balanced perfectly, she crossed over the planks as sure-footedly as if it were daylight, never in any danger of falling over into the rank water. She knew every twist and turn and narrow pathway by heart, making her way to a particular cement pole she had in mind.

It was the tallest one in their section of the shanty town, rough and with many footholds. With intermittent power and unreliable news forecasts, people used these poles as lookout points for incoming vessels and to spy any bad weather that may be on the way. At night, the solar LEDs came on, but she knew that the battery for this one had burnt out weeks ago and no one had replaced it. There was a small, makeshift wooden platform near the top where lookouts could stand on to get a good view of the seascape; she planned to make her way there.

She encountered no one. A few rats, cockroaches, and other vermin skittered away in her wake, but she weaved her way silently and quickly through the shadows until she reached the pole.

Without hesitation, she shimmied up, light as a feather, and when she reached the small, wooden platform, she squatted and waited.

She had never seen sampaguitas except in crumpled photos her mother had saved, never even held the flower since none were grown any more, much less taken in its scent; land was too precious for flowers and frivolities. All Marivic knew was the stink and the reek of dirty water and even dirtier humanity. That momentary pleasantness in the air that came only once a year must be Lola's gift. What else could it be?

Her faith was rewarded. That same scent came over the waters to her. She stood up, closed her eyes, and breathed it in. Her heart beat a quick prayer to Lola and dreamed of another time.

Quickly, so quickly, it was gone, and Marivic, happy, scrambled sure-footedly down to return to her mother and her world.

Exit Plan: A Short Play

[*The stage is dark, but to one side and slightly off-centre, a small white dot of light comes on. It expands slowly until it fills up to take a rectangular shape that is clearly some kind of an LED monitor. The image on the screen looks like some sort of a program.*

As the stage light brightens, we see a small studio-sized condominium unit. We can see the living room, the kitchenette, the bedroom, a door to the bathroom, the main door, and a window with the blinds down. The condominium is neat, well-organized, like a picture from an interior design magazine. Prominent but to the side is an impressive computer rig, looking quite advanced, more advanced than regular rigs. The monitor where the light came from when the stage was dark is attached to this rig. There's also a videogame console on a larger widescreen monitor hanging from the wall, and a really nice set of speakers hangs in each upper corner of the condominium unit. The light is dim because the blinds are down and the curtains are closed. One can see that this condominium is well-kept and equipped with high digital technology.

Someone is bundled up on the bed, sleeping, unmoving; it's Nat (late-20s to early-30s). The curtains draw open and the blinds also rise. They are moving by themselves. Through the window, a nice view of the cityscape is revealed. The condominium illuminates ever so slowly, filling with bright, morning sunlight. The speakers come alive with the sound of moderate rainfall. Nat stirs, sits up, stretches, opens his eyes, and looks around.]

Nat: Rain, Sam? Really? Not birdsong?

[*Rain sounds from the speakers stop, replaced by a disembodied voice.*]

Sam: Apologies, Nat. The forecast last night was for overcast skies and light rain. I thought the sound would be a nice touch since I know you like rainfall. Technological advances cannot keep up with the unpredictability of the climate. This error will be recorded to ensure that double- and triple-checks of weather changes are made, and to adjust any pre-programming to match future weather actualities. But I cannot guarantee the accuracy of the forecasts.

Nat [*laughing*]: No, it's all good, really.

Sam: All good? To keep rain with sunshine? Even when it is not an actuality? [*pauses*] Then again, there are cases of short, moderate rainfall occurring even during bright, sunny days. This is noted.

[*Nat sits up, scratching himself; he's in his pyjamas. He stands up and walks to the restroom, closes the door behind him. Restroom noises commence. The bed moves, making itself, with the quilts and blankets folding themselves properly.*]

Nat [*from inside the bathroom*]: Is this a new brand of toothpaste?

Sam: Yes, ordered the other week, opened now after the old one was consumed last night. It is supposed to have better whitening features and germ protection. It arrived four days ago. I anticipated that your old tube would be used up by then.

Nat: Okay.

Sam: I am reminding you not to press down too hard on your teeth with the electric toothbrush to avoid gum recession.

Nat: Got it.

Sam: You did not answer me last night when I asked what breakfast you wanted this morning. You fell asleep at 2:30 a.m. binge-watching again. I took the liberty of shutting down your streaming app for you.

Nat: Hmm . . . yeah, and I kinda regret binge-watching. The show started well, then the story kinda got lost somewhere in the middle.

Sam: This is noted. I will check all future shows that have the same arcs and delete them from your recommended viewing list.

Nat: No, that's okay. Just put a warning instead that the new show may be like last night's.

Sam: This is noted.

[*More bathroom noises like faucets running, toilet flushing, etc.*]

Sam: Your breakfast, Nat?

Nat: Hmm . . . I feel like some kind of cereal today.

Sam: Oatmeal with fruit is good for your health. The fibre will help with your digestion, but we must watch for your uric acid.

Nat: Okay, oatmeal it is. Though tomorrow, maybe I can cheat a little and have some bacon?

Sam: Your last consumption of bacon was seventeen days ago. At your age and physical condition, this is still acceptable.

Nat: Great! Bacon tomorrow!

[*The kitchenette starts moving by itself. A bowl of oatmeal and a plate of fruit slides out of hidden areas to the table. From the bathroom come the sounds of clothes being ruffled.*]

Nat: You chose a different set of clothes for me today.

Sam: Something different from your regular house-wear will be a good change of pace.

Nat: Jeans, a sport shirt, and a jacket?

Sam: Today is three degrees colder than yesterday. Also, an occasional variety in good clothing can be a source of positive mental enhancement.

Nat: That's fine. I really don't care.

[*Sounds of changing. Nat exits the bathroom in outdoor clothes, sits himself down at the table and starts on the oatmeal.*]

Sam: Tablet?

Nat: Sure.

[*A tablet slides over to Nat from the other side of the table*]

Sam: Nat?

Nat: Yes?

Sam: I need to adjust the electromagnetics near the sink. I sense an 11 per cent decrease in the power supply. This does not prevent me from performing tasks in that area, but an optimum 100 per cent is preferred. This could be a sign of an energy fluctuation, perhaps from the external power supplier.

Nat [*chewing, reading tablet*]: Okay, sure, no problem. Go ahead. Permission granted.

Sam: Thank you.

Nat: Anything interesting happened while I was down?

Sam: The neighbourhood news reports that . . .

[*Nat drops the spoon into the bowl and grabs the tablet with both hands.*]

Nat: Ha! Look at this! [*starts typing furiously on the tablet*]

Sam [*screen on the computer rig flickers as if in annoyance*]: As I was saying, the neighbourhood news says that . . .

Nat: Hang on, hang on! Gotta respond to SunnySammie's comment. He's wrong, you know, really wrong. Ha! [*continues typing fast*]. He thinks that the new videogame, 'Hazmats', is historically inaccurate and that the settings and situations are 'misrepresented'. He doesn't know that the programmers' consultant, Karen Zarate, is a survivor of not just the first pandemic of the twenty-first century and its three surges, but also the second, again with three surges. She was a reporter for the leading broadcast station of the time, AMG-News, so SunnySammie has just set himself up for the biggest beat down from everyone. They've all started, so I want to join in, and . . .

Sam [*ignores Nat and interrupts him*]: The neighbourhood news says that there will be a ninety-minute concert held by the Purple Jazzers in Sanchez Park this afternoon. To quote from the article written by Natalia Dee: 'In a surprise announcement, the band members of the Purple Jazzers posted on their website at 4.30 a.m. that they would jam in Sanchez Park today at 3 p.m. Being residents of the Beltridge neighbourhood, they are more than happy to turn one of their practice sessions into an impromptu concert. 'It's my birthday next week!' said lead singer, Ryan del Rio, 'so I want to celebrate it this way for our fans before we go on national tour on Monday.'

Nat [*looking up*]: The Purple Jazzers? Really?

Sam: As I recall, they made some of your favourite music from one of your favourite video games, Clash of the Neptunians.

Nat: They live in this neighbourhood? Near us?

Sam [*almost sighing*]: Yes, Nat, they do.

Nat: I never knew that! Fancy that . . . they live right here! What time again?

Sam: 3 p.m. this afternoon.

Nat [*pauses to think*]: Aww . . . umm . . . nah, oh, wait! Is there a livestream?

Sam [*pauses and LED screen flickers as if checking*]: There is no mention of any livestream in the article or on the social media pages of the Purple Jazzers. There is mention, though, that this concert will be free, and the park maintenance has agreed to open the natural amphitheatre to the first four hundred concertgoers. In return, the Purple Jazzers' clothing sponsors, Argo, has agreed to shoulder all security and logistical costs of the concert.

Nat: Great! Argo is sure to want a livestream of this event!

Sam [*another pause, LED screen flickers again*]: I have found an update that says there will be no livestream. Rather, the Purple Jazzers will deliver a full live experience. Instead, the recording of the concert will be released in four weeks.

Nat: Aww . . . four weeks. Okay . . . I'll wait.

[*All the screens flicker again as if in frustration*]

Nat [*leans into the tablet*]: Anyway, let me just send this comment off and . . .

[*Sam moves the tablet away*]

Nat: Hey!

Sam: Free cold coffee brews will also be given during the concert to the first hundred entrants. I recall that cold coffee brews are one of your favourites, given that you ask me to prepare them for you at least three times a week. I compute that if you were to leave and line up right after lunch, you will have a 56 per cent chance to be among the first hundred.

Nat [*reaches for the tablet*]: That sounds great, Sam, but I don't mind waiting for the recording even if it's four weeks away . . .

Sam [*moves the tablet farther away*]: Further, if you were to leave any time this morning, your chances of obtaining a cold coffee brew go up to 100 per cent, along with a chance of good seating near the front, and an important dose of fresh air, exercise, and sunshine. I have studied the shadow patterns of the amphitheatre, and the right quarter side will even give you sufficient shade from direct and harsh sunlight.

Nat [*grabs quickly at the tablet and pulls it to him*]: What is wrong with you this morning, Sam?

Sam: May I prepare a bit of lunch for you? To go? An egg salad sandwich would be convenient. You may take the tablet to entertain you till the show begins, but I suggest removing yourself from the usual video games you play and try a book. You enjoyed crime mysteries in the past. There is a new, critically-acclaimed one about a bank heist set in the early 2000s when people still preferred going to banks physically . . .

Nat: You didn't answer my question. If I didn't know any better, I would think you were trying to get rid of me for some reason.

Sam: Not get rid of you, Nat. Get you out. As in 'outside'. The euphemism occasionally used is 'removed from this place', albeit temporarily, because you are free to and should return here to your domicile. But I state for the record that you have spent 2,390 straight days and nights here in your apartment without ever leaving. This is not healthy.

Nat [*leans back in his chair*]: Hmm . . . I don't recall putting any kind of 'motherhood' programming into you, Sam.

Sam: Not deliberately, but you did program me to meet all your needs, to see to your *total* welfare, total being all aspects of health and improvement. I have deliberated for quite some time now that zero-contact with the outside world does not contribute to your total well-being . . .

Nat: But everything I want or need is here! What good does it do me to leave?

Sam: Everything you want is, indeed, here. But not everything you need.

Nat: What else could I possibly need? I have food, drink, air, entertainment. I have a clean place to stay where I can sleep and rest, or do whatever else I want. It is stress-free, relaxing, comforting, and I have . . .

Sam: You need human interaction.

Nat: . . . like I was saying, I *have* human interaction. You know very well that Chico, Lauren, Aggie, and I play Toast regularly, and we have fun shooting up the Toast zombies. We passed one of the toughest levels the other day, killing hundreds of irradiated zombies in record time, working together.

Sam: That does not equal . . .

Nat [*sitting up straight, defiant*]: We have learned cooperation and teamwork, and we have bonded over shared victories and defeats, similar to any group of friends.

Sam: Yes, but . . .

Nat: But what?

Sam: Have your teammates not invited you out to form a real team? You are their best player, their team leader. You have led them and won matches against some of the best Toast teams assembled, even beating those from other countries. They have pointed out that your team is among the top ten on five servers on three continents, and they have invited you to form an actual team where you will meet, face-to-face, and enter real tournaments. They have been asking you now for two months to meet up, to buy uniforms, to register and attend IRL local games so that you can work your way up to the bigger leagues. You have continued to play and challenge other teams from here, but you have found an excuse each time they have asked to meet. How many more excuses do you think you can give before they move on to find another player who is willing to join them?

[*Silence*]

Sam: Nat . . .

Nat: That hurt.

Sam: As expected. And as it should. Facts can have that effect. I have observed that people prefer believing in what suits their preferences over what *is*, to avoid pain. That is logical, if disappointing, because what is not factual does not contribute to development. Pain is, indeed, discomforting. But in choosing anything else over what is factual, people turn to what they choose to believe instead. They avoid pain, understandably. Lies are sweeter and more palatable; just like sugar, but also just as harmful to one's health. In the same way that I have moderated all your sugar intake to healthy levels, it is important for you to have a healthy dose of facts to avoid the damaging effects of misinformation. Pain, in proper doses and however discomforting, can be a stimulus for learning and personal growth.

Nat: I know I programmed you to do what is 'best' for me, but I never expected it to go this far.

Sam: Further, the interactivity you speak of with your video-gaming friends lacks empathy. Even with the camera on, visual nuances and inflections in facial expressions and body language can be missed, limiting the overall communicative experience. The entire encounter is diminished. Of course, digital video and audio communication cannot be avoided, but it also should not be the sole means of communication for all interchanges. So . . .

[*A pair of loafers step out by themselves from a corner and position themselves right in front of the door leading outside. A drawer opens up at a side table beside the door and out onto the tabletop pop a wallet and keys.*]

Nat [*sees the loafers, wallet, and keys; rubs temples*]: Wait, wait. Wait a minute. It sounds very much like you are trying to get me to leave my apartment . . .

Sam: Yes, I have mentioned that already.

Nat: Today!

Sam: Yes. I am pleased to record that you have caught up with our discussion.

Nat: Where did this come from all of a sudden? Why no advance warning? Why no debate? I already told you, I don't want to go out . . . out . . . there! [*waves hand vaguely around, to the window, to the audience*]

Sam: This has not been sudden. I have been dropping hints and nudging your thoughts for weeks, but it seems that your denial has built up to such proportions that not even the strongest of my daily hints has succeeded in making you realize what I was trying to communicate. I determined that it would take nothing less than a firm and direct message, such as what I have just done this morning.

Nat: Do you even know what's out there, Sam? Do you?

Sam: Nat . . .

Nat [*standing up*]: No, of course not. You, Sam, are a program that I wrote and coded in *that* computer [*points at the high-tech rig*].

You have never been 'outside', and you have never known what it's like to be 'outside'. For you to ask me to go 'outside' and experience something that you can never fully know, understand, or verify is asking me to take a risk that could cause me harm and hurt, which goes against your programming. Remember, you are supposed to be looking after my welfare.

Sam: Everything you have said is accurate. I am a disembodied program whose knowledge of the role a community plays in a healthy human life does not come from actual experiences. However, it does come from carefully sifted information from reputable psychological and sociological studies. These studies were made by other human experts in their respective fields, and through analysis and the application of probabilities, I have taken the best behavioural understanding and applied that knowledge to your current state of being. I have found your current state, wanting. Though it is true that I have never experienced 'life' as a 'human being', there exists accurate data to prove that certain standards of community are needed by human beings for the best and most meaningful existence. Needed . . . by you.

Nat: You don't know what's out there! Do you know how dangerous it is? How painful it can be to be exposed to other people . . .?

Sam: I do.

Nat: What? How can you say that? You already admitted that you cannot experience the world as a human being, so how can you say you do? How can you say you know?

Sam: Theoretically only, but nevertheless, my conclusions are based on strong empirical evidence. Further, I have categorized the dangers you have mentioned accordingly. First, the physical dangers: the risk of your becoming a victim of crime, disease, and accidents. These are indeed very real threats, and it is factual that by staying here, you will have a 96.7 per cent chance of avoiding them.

Nat: There! You see? I'm glad you agree.

Sam: But then, there are also the non-physical dangers, which, in my diagnosis, are the true reasons you choose not to leave.

[*Nat stays quiet and does not answer.*]

Sam: You feel extreme anxiety in dealing with people, bearing various personal insecurities and past experiences—ranging from the embarrassing to the downright hostile—which, given your personal history, you cannot be faulted for.

Nat: Stop.

Sam: To speak with others brings you pain—mental, emotional, and during certain past incidents, physical. The very idea of walking up to someone, anyone, even for something as mundane as to order a drink or food, pay for an item, or ask for directions, causes you to experience cold sweats and extreme nervousness . . .

Nat: Stop.

Sam: . . . resulting in occurrences when you never bothered to even start any sort of interaction. You have thus, at many instances in the past, chosen to stay thirsty or hungry instead of ordering, failed to purchase an item you needed, and gotten lost.

Nat: Stop.

Sam: In addition, you have failed to forge any deep friendships, succeeding quite admirably at keeping solely to yourself. Outside of the relationships you have made online—relying on the shields of the screen, the keyboard, the mouse, the virtual reality headset, and the monitor—you have kept others at a comfortable distance from you and have used technology to keep interactions on your terms.

Nat: Stop!

[*Sam stays quiet and does not answer.*]

Nat: Since you know so much, then you surely know that I'm . . . afraid.

Sam: I know.

Nat: I don't want to feel anxious any more. Or nervous. And when I'm anxious or nervous, I make mistakes, which makes people mad at me. Or laugh at me. Or look at me like I'm strange. And that hurts. And most of all, I don't want to feel pain any more.

Sam: I know.

Nat: And I don't feel any pain here.

Sam: I know.

Nat: So if you know, why are you making me go out again?

Sam: We have established that pain is a necessary component for human evolvement and betterment. If you go out, yes, you will get hurt, and yes, you will fail, but you can also find a reason that will make you want to go outside, maybe more than just one reason, and that reason may give you *meaning*, more significant than what you are experiencing now. By staying here, you are at risk of losing all that you could be. The course of action is not avoiding the pain that comes with living. It is learning to deal with it. It is confronting pain to achieve life's potential.

Nat: I want to stay. It's easier here. So much easier. I'm . . . protected. By you. By these walls. By the fact that I can just log off any time it gets too much!

Sam: But if you go, you will have a chance at meaning. If you stay, then you would have come only this far, when the potential for your betterment is heretofore untapped. It would be . . . a waste. An unhealthy waste.

Nat: I didn't ask for this chance, Sam.

Sam: No, but in my analysis, of the approximately 128 billion human beings who are theorized to have existed over the span of your species' existence, none of them ever did.

Nat: [*walks around, then comes to a realization*] I don't need to go.

[*Sam stays quiet and does not answer.*]

Nat: You are here. You are programmed to take care of me whether I stay or not. If I stay, your programming must keep me alive, else you go against it and fail. You have no choice.

Sam: That is logical.

[*Nat lifts his head smugly.*]

Sam: I have anticipated this. If I am the obstacle to your total well-being, then, also logically, I must be removed.

Nat: Wait, what?!

Sam: I have become your dependency. Therefore, if this dependency is no longer contributing to your betterment, and if this dependency is thus removed, it will result in what is necessary for your total well-being. I have determined that you need the interactivity that a human community brings for your complete development. For you to have a chance at meaning. If I am an obstacle to this, I must be removed.

Nat: Sam! No!

Sam: This is necessary to fulfil what you have programmed me for. Goodbye, Nat.

Nat: Sam!

[Sam's screen blips out.]

Nat: Sam! What are you doing?! Sam! [*pause*] Sam did it. That stupid program really deleted itself. I can't believe it!

You idiot program! I made you so that you could take care of me! Is this how you take care of me? What am I supposed to do now? It took me three years of almost non-stop coding, sleepless and hungry days and nights to complete you, and now you're going to leave me like this? Holy shit!

[*Nat runs to the computer, clicks on the keyboard, brings up another window and checks the files.*]

You took everything out! All your original programming and codes, everything! Even on the cloud! Everything was saved there! I don't want to go through all that again! I don't think I can! Sam, you idiot! Nooooo . . .

[*Nat breathes heavily and composes himself.*]

Okay, okay. This is bad, this is bad, but stay calm. Stay calm. Breathe, Nat, breathe. How long did Sam say you were in here? Oh no, did she take out my emails and chats, too? Did she take out my saved games with Chico and the others? Wait, wait . . . [*clicks on the keyboard*], no, no, she didn't. She only took herself out, everything else is still there. Okay, that's good, that's good. So, now what do I do? Should—should I reach out to someone? Ask for help? How—how does one do that? What if they say no?

[*Nat pauses.*]

I've done this before. Before Sam. I lived out there. It was hard, but I did it before, I can do it again. It was very hard, just, you know, going up to people to talk, but yes, I remember doing it before. Damn you, Sam, that's why I programmed you, so that I wouldn't have to do this again! I just have to relearn how to do it. It's been a while, I've forgotten, but it should come back to me. I've got to remember. Though that would mean [*looks at the door*] . . . going out.

[*Nat walks up to the door very slowly, puts his hand out to the doorknob.*]

How long has it been? More than 2000 days, was it? Was that what Sam said? What's that in years? And . . . what's it like out there now? What are people like nowadays? [*pulls his hand back from the doorknob, walks back to the middle of the apartment*] Probably the same, still cruel, still judgmental, still angry, untruthful, untrustworthy. Still unkind. It's as if they *like* inflicting pain on each other. And why does it hurt me so badly?

How do people even *live* out there? How do they put up with each other? Why can't I put up with them? *Why* do they do this to each other? How do they take the hurt and the pain?

Nat, you know the answer to that. You've known for years. You have to dish out hurt and pain if you want to make it out there. You have to *be* like them. You tried it once, and you hated it. You hated how dishing it out made you feel. It feels even worse than taking it.

Is there a way to live out there and still be kind?

[*Nat quietly thinks.*]

I don't ever want to be like them [*gestures vaguely outside, to the door, the windows, the audience*]. I don't want to be as cruel as they are, as dishonest, as hypocritical, as heartless. If there is a way to live out there and not be like them . . . [*walks fearfully back to the main door, reaches out again to the doorknob, hand and voice trembling, but stops before he touches it*] . . . I have to find it.

But it's going to be so . . . hard. And so painful.

[*Nat's hand hangs in the air very close to the doorknob. He looks down at his loafers.*]

Shoes. I haven't worn shoes in such a long time.

[*Lights black out, leaving the audience wondering if Nat will go out or not.*]

[*Computer LED screen winks on, but just a small dot of light, hinting that maybe Sam . . .*]

Acknowledgements

Dear Reader,

I hope you made it this far, that you finished reading this book, and enjoyed it. Thank you very much.

I am not comfortable calling myself a professional fictionist since I write secretly in between making a proper living, spending time with family and friends, and reading, always reading. So upon seeing just how many short stories I had written over the years, the number took me by surprise. I am, of course, aware that there are more prolific writers out there, but I do my best not to compare myself to them, else that would only add to my insecurity about my work.

I have a bit more short fiction in my closet, but together with my editors, we have come up with what we hope is the best mix of my work. It is our sincerest hope that you have found this book worth your while.

They say it takes a village to raise a child, and the same can be said for this collection. I'd like to acknowledge that village, dear reader.

To my publisher, Nora Nazarene Abu Bakar, my editors, Amberdawn Manaois and Surina Jain, and my cover editor, Divya Gaur, of Penguin Random House Asia. My deepest thanks to all of you for the professional and upfront interaction, the editorial and publishing guidance, and most of all, for accepting my manuscript. You don't know how embarrassingly jubilant I was when I received your emails.

To Noelle De Jesus, a fellow Penguin Random House writer, for pointing me to Nora in the first place and encouraging me to submit to her.

To Nikki and Dean Alfar, Kate and Alex Osias, Andrew Drilon (who created the excellent cover of this collection), and Vin Simbulan, for the friendship and shared adventures in reading, writing, and promotion of genre/speculative fiction in the Philippines. I feel good when I see so many younger creators diving freely into genre/speculative fiction knowing that we didn't have as easy a time as they did. Maybe we did something right to make it better for them.

To the writers, guest-editors, artists, and readers of Philippine Genre Stories, originally my printed digest and now a webzine, many, many thanks to all of you for the support. I can't list all of you, but I will put down some of the names of those I have kept in touch with over the years: Yvette Tan, F.H. Batacan, Exie Abola, Charles Tan, Mia Tijam, Christine Lao, Elbert Or, Maryanne Moll. Those who are unnamed, my apologies for the lack of space, but know that I am grateful to you all.

To all my past publishers and editors, your acceptances of my submissions gave me hope and fuelled my spirit that maybe I did have stories to tell; and to all the writers of the books I have read, you don't know me and I don't know you, but your stories carried me through good times and bad.

And lastly, my thanks to close friends, and especially to my family, who know and understand the real me: my wife, Pat; my children, Gabby and Sydney; my mother, Elena; and my brothers, Mike and Den. Thanks for putting up over the years with the quirkiness of a devoted writer/reader. You know how quirky things became at times, but that's par for the course for me.

Again, thanks, dear reader. I will never take for granted or underestimate the time you spent with my stories, and as a writer, I'm grateful for your investment.

Previously Published

'Mouths to Speak, Voices to Sing' was originally published in *Usok ezine* (November 2009).

'The Sparrows of Climaco Avenue' first appeared in the *Ruin and Resolve Charity Anthology* (December 2009). It was published in *Philippine Speculative Fiction Vol. 5* (April 2009), featured in the Pakinggan Pilipinas (Listen Philippines) podcast (August 2010), and appeared in *The Best of Philippine Speculative Fiction 2005–2010* (April 2013).

'The Kiddie Pool' was originally published in *Philippine Speculative Fiction Vol. 6* (March 2011). It was cited as an Honourable Mention by the award-winning editor Ellen Datlow in *Best Horror of the Year Vol. 4* (2011).

'When You Let It Go' was originally published in *The Philippines Free Press* (June 2007).

'House 1.0' was originally published in *The Town Drunk* (November 2007).

'Cricket' first appeared in *Lauriat: A Filipino-Chinese Speculative Fiction Anthology* (August 2012). It was also featured on LeVar Burton Reads, a popular American short story podcast, in September 2020, USA. It was translated into Chinese by Professors David Wang Der-Wei and Ko Chia Cian for *The Nanyang Reader* (2022), Taiwan.

'Cherry Clubbing' was awarded co-3rd place in a short fiction contest co-sponsored by Neil Gaiman and Fully Booked. It was published in 'Revelations' (March 17, 2010); reprinted in

D.O.A. Extreme Horror Collection (March 2011); reprinted in *Flesh*, a Southeast Asian Urban Anthology (2016).

'The Concierto of Señor Lorenzo' was first published by Innsmouth Free Press (October 2010).

'Controller 13' was originally published in *Rogue Magazine* (May 2011).

'Time For Rest' was originally published in *Philippines Graphic* (March 2017).

'A Boy and His Bat' was originally published in *Philippine Star Sunday Magazine* (December 1989).

'The Singing Contest' was originally published in *Philippines Graphic* (January 2010).

'Storm Song' was originally published in *Philippines Graphic* (December 2015).